Advance Praise

"Darby takes on loss and grief with a subtle wisdom. Hers is a narrative for our times."

— Afaa M. Weaver, author of *A Fire in the Hills*

"Jane Darby's taut novella speaks to the depths of life-altering loss and the power of the human spirit to transform it. *All That Remains* will keep you on the edge of your seat and break your heart."

— Tom Lagasse, author and poet

"*All That Remains* explodes off the page with domestic tension. Darby delivers a richly slanted view of contemporary American life."

— Bill Ratner, author of *Fear of Fish*

"Darby weaves her story in clear and lyrically honed prose reminiscent of Updike."

— Davyne Verstandig, poet and teacher

"Jane Darby is a master storyteller. I knew I was in good hands from page one."

— Andy Christie, The Moth Radio Hour

All That Remains

All That Remains

Jane Darby

Apprentice House Press
Loyola University Maryland

Library of Congress Control Number: 2025931692

First Edition

Casebound ISBN: 978-1-62720-548-1
Paperback ISBN: 978-1-62720-549-8
Ebook ISBN: 978-1-62720-550-4

Design by Apprentice House Press
Editorial Development by Mac Ferrone
Promotion Development by Aminah Murray
Author Photo by David Darby

Published by Apprentice House Press

Apprentice
House Press
Loyola University Maryland

Loyola University Maryland
4501 N. Charles Street, Baltimore, MD 21210
410.617.5265
www.ApprenticeHouse.com
info@ApprenticeHouse.com

For my north star, David and for our planets, Nick and Dana.

April 2006
Thursday

1

"I wouldn't wait until the weekend. Why not head up this afternoon? By yourself." Richard stirred cream into his coffee and wiped the spoon clean with a paper napkin. "What do you think?"

"Yes," Anna said, trying to plumb this peace offering. "I could do that."

"You said you wanted to have some time alone. It will be good for you. Fresh air. Take a walk in the woods. That's why we bought the place. A little peace and quiet, no?" He smiled. "You can get started on your garden."

Anna sipped her coffee, wincing at the heat. She couldn't blame him for wanting to get rid of her. Last night's fight had ended in retreat: he, to the bedroom and she, to Ben's old room, now a den. Curled up on the divan, she listened to the sounds of Richard getting ready for bed: click of a light switch, rush of water in the sink, sounds of an intimate, shared life, so calm and deliberate that each was another stone in the wall rising between them.

But here at breakfast with sunlight streaming through the window and coffee cooling in their mugs, civility had returned and along with it, a fragile truce. "Yes," she repeated. "I could do that."

"Good. I'm working late tonight anyway. I'll catch a train Friday evening. You'll pick me up at the station?" He smiled at her, eyebrows raised as if there were any question.

"Of course."

It wasn't until she was driving up the Palisades that she realized Richard was right. The city had barely dropped away, and already she felt a lift in spirits. Trees flashed by, still winter-naked though some were shot with early sprays of green. Yellow Forsythia bloomed along the side of the road. Up the rise and around the bend, she passed a small lake tucked into the landscape like a secret. Farther up, the road cut past cliffs glistening with the spring thaw. The ascent peaked and suddenly below her: a Walmart. A Chuck E. Cheese. More stores were under construction, wrapped in a white membrane with the big, blue words *Tyvek, Tyvek, Tyvek*. This was surrounded by a vast parking lot with rows of cars where crops once grew.

She needed a shovel. If she was going to cut sod and build a fence for the garden, she would need a shovel. And some chicken wire. Stakes for fence posts. Work gloves. She tried to think it through, to cast her mind ahead to what might be needed. Without warning, bile rose to her mouth, and she gasped.

What might be needed.

She pressed her lips together and swallowed the thought whole.

Pay attention. Needle-nosed pliers with a built-in wire cutter.

She took the exit to Walmart.

The vastness of the store was a shock after the cramped aisles of Manhattan markets. Anna pushed a cart that could house a family of four past a bin of Easter candy marked half-off. Over the loudspeaker a voice squawked that chicken tenders were buy one, get one free in the frozen food section. Everyone was in a state of fatigued awe. Anna watched a worn-out couple in their late twenties worry each other over whether they should put a wide-screen TV on layaway. A toddler with a snot-crusted nose and raw upper lip rocked and keened in the child's seat of the cart while a five-year-old boy or girl—Anna wasn't sure with that haircut—pulled on the woman's arm, chanting indecipherable demands. Suddenly, the man swung his head around to the child. "Tyler, if you don't shut up, I'll give you something to shut up about."

Anna looked away.

The selection in Gardening Supplies was slim since it was so early in the season. There were some shovels and hand tools. An entire row was devoted to poisons for pests. If she had wanted to, she could've bought a reflective blue sphere perched on a Grecian pedestal made of durable plastic. She couldn't believe they didn't sell chicken wire. At least they had deer netting. She angled a couple of rolls into her cart.

On her way out of the store, she paused by the vending machines. When Ben was little, it had been impossible to pass them without stopping. They would be walking down Broadway, in a hurry, as usual, to get him to school and her to work, and there the vending machines would be, banked against the storefront of a deli or a news shop. Without warning, Ben would dart over and start fiddling with the mechanisms.

Mom, can I have a quarter?

No, Ben. Come on.

C'mon, Mom. Please. Just one.

What is it you want?

That. That plastic thing.

Ben, it's nothing. It's junk. It's landfill.

It's a thing, *Mom!*

He was always a sucker for The Claw, a glassed-in chamber filled with stuffed animals, bouncy balls, and cheap digital watches that worked for about five minutes. For a dollar a pop, you could guide a three-fingered mechanical hand to lower, grasp, and retrieve whatever your heart desired. Ben always pestered her for that one. She tried to tell him. She even let him do it once to show him it was nothing but a cheat. But out of sheer, dumb luck he managed to pull up a stuffed something, a green alien with huge almond-shaped eyes that glowed in the dark. From that day on, he was hooked.

Anna pushed her cart over to The Claw. Of course, there was nothing in it she wanted, but she fished some quarters from her coat pocket and dropped them into the slot. The chamber lit up as a tinny rendition of *Under the Sea* buzzed through the speakers. She studied the jumble of plush fur and plastic, steered the claw over to a purple teddy bear, fine-tuned the positioning, and pushed the button. The claw descended over the bear's head and pulled up. The mechanism had no more strength in it than an old woman's arthritic hand. The fingers slipped over the bear and returned home empty handed. What had she expected?

It was night by the time Anna pulled up to the house. The footpath to the porch was so dark and unfamiliar that she had to toe her way along the flagstone and up the broad wooden steps leading to the door. She felt with her fingers for the lock and guided her key into it. *Entry by braille*, she thought as she pushed against the heavy door and pawed the wall to switch on the lights.

It was an old house, an Adirondack-style hunter's lodge built in the 1930s with a stone fireplace, vaulted ceilings, exposed beams and rafters, and plenty of taxidermy left by the previous owner. A moose's head, mangy with age, hung high over the hearth. From the moment he saw it, Richard had fallen in love with the house with its long, gravel driveway and the wooded hills that surrounded it. "A real find," he whispered to Anna when the realtor turned her back. "The real thing." Once it was theirs, he took to calling it "The Lodge," or, when he was feeling particularly grand, "The Manor." Anna referred to it as "The House of Heads," to which Richard always admonished, "Don't be ugly."

It was grand and it was the real thing, but it was also terribly gloomy. The timbered walls absorbed light. From the shadows, deer looked down with glass eyes empty of life. A scent of musty, old fur and wood filled the air. Anna set her bags by the sofa and flicked on as many lamps as she could find, but still the room felt dark and heavy. A tomb. She decided to light a fire.

There was plenty of firewood—the caretaker had seen to that. But Anna, a city dweller for most of her life, hadn't paid attention when Richard lit their first fire several weeks ago. She had been sitting right in that armchair, drifting off as usual, sinking herself with her thoughts.

She could not shake her astonishment that life continued. Even after all this time—more than a year—something in her refused to understand it. How was it possible that she could sit in an armchair and watch her husband fumble about with matches? How was it possible that when he struck the match, it lit? Shouldn't the world stop? Shouldn't the laws of nature be suspended? How could a man who had lost his only child still manage to light a fire?

Anna had been married to Richard for twenty-five years, yet she did not understand him. He possessed the gift of taking life in stride, while she took each new blow as if it might be her last. Even through the initial shock of the phone call, the subdued voice of a stranger on the other end, the interminable drive to Philadelphia, the awful sight of Ben in the morgue—still and waxy, not really Ben at all, more the absence of Ben—through all of that, Richard had held it together. And in the days that followed, he made the calls, the arrangements; he spoke at the memorial service, while Anna simply shut down.

A couple of weeks after the service when there was nothing left to do, Anna found Richard lying in bed, pulled into a tight fetal curl. She lay down next to him, cupped his back with her body, and snaked her arm around his belly and up his chest. But he was stone: silent and cold. Finally, she got up and left him to himself. She spent the night on the sofa. The next morning, she woke to the sounds of Richard making coffee. When he brought her a cup and set it on a coaster on the coffee table, she knew he had finished mourning and was resolved to get on with the business of living.

Anna wadded sheets of newspaper into balls and arranged them on the grate.

Well, how hard could it be? All you have to do is light a match. People light fires all the time. Check the flue, for God's sake. Don't smoke yourself out of the place.

She pulled a box of matches off the stone mantle and lit the newspaper. Smoke twisted up, and then a flame sparked and spread. The wads of paper brightened and curled, and soon the whole pile was blazing. She grabbed a piece of wood and threw it on top. The fire hushed and died, leaving only paper ash and an utterly cold log. Anna wadded more newspapers, lit more matches, blew into the flames, but the log refused to catch. *Jesus Christ,* she thought. *Can't you even light a fire?*

You suck at this, Mom.

Stop it, Ben.

No. Really. You do.

Anna closed the screen on the fireplace and went to bed early.

2

The productive hum of the office dropped to a murmur after the nine-to-fivers departed. Richard remained at his desk. He had to put the final touches on tomorrow's taste test trials for a mocha raspberry snack cake. He'd checked in with Tech. Had a few more calls to make to Chicago and the West Coast. Double and triple-checked *everything*. For some time now he had grown inexplicably anxious about the work, sitting in the conference room with the execs from the client company and watching the results through live webcast feeds. With all his experience, these trials should be a breeze, but lately he'd been making rookie mistakes that embarrassed him and made him wonder what else he'd screwed up.

To compound the pressure, there was a new boss to impress—a Brit named Rupert Simon. Richard had to watch himself. The other day he caught himself referring to him as Simon Rupert. He seemed a decent enough chap, once you got past his hail-fellow-well-met manner. That and the fact that at his last post he'd slashed the staff by twenty percent.

Richard's secretary, a diligent, joyless woman, offered to stay late as well but he let her go, grateful for a stretch of quiet, uninterrupted time. He worked well into the evening, long enough to greet the cleaning crew and shut his door on the whir of vacuum cleaners and foreign chatter.

It occurred to him that he should call Anna. See that she had gotten in all right, but he decided he'd phone her from the apartment later. By then she'd be tired, maybe already in bed. They could keep their conversation brief and avoid another fight. Instead, he left a message at the caretaker's, instructing him to head over to the property early tomorrow with the rototiller. What a surprise for Anna! Hours of daunting, backbreaking labor saved. She really had no idea what she was in for with this garden idea of hers.

The air was cool and brisk when Richard finally stepped out of the lobby onto Tenth Avenue. Apartment buildings glowed with the nightlight of people in for the evening. He decided to walk the thirty-odd blocks home, if his knees would allow it. His doctor had recommended that he get a little exercise. Maybe he would sleep better.

As he joined the stream of pedestrians heading north, he calculated: two dollars each way on the bus, four dollars a day, twenty dollars a week, eighty-six dollars a month, an impressive one thousand, thirty-two dollars a year. Over a period of ten years, not counting compounded interest or rate hikes by the MTA, he could realize a savings of ten thousand, three hundred twenty dollars.

The rhythm of his calculations matched his pace: *the money, the money, the money.* The money was good now. Had been for some time. He was earning more than he ever imagined he would, and with markets in Asia opening up, he ought to make a good showing this year. Yet, he could not shake worries of rising fuel costs, volatility in corn futures, whispers of layoffs in the regional offices. Earthquakes, floods, and pestilence. Civil unrest. Terrorist attacks. You just never know.

There was some kind of commotion up ahead. People were gathered on the corner, their conversations dropped, their attention focused on a single point. Two cars—a yellow taxicab and a gun-metal gray SUV—rested at odd angles in the middle of the intersection. The right front end of the SUV was crumpled, the headlight shattered. The driver, a hulk of a man in a t-shirt—*I ♥ New York*—opened his door, cursing as soon as his feet hit the pavement. Richard saw a wide-eyed young woman in the back seat with a baby in her arms. She watched the man as he strode around to the damaged fender and slammed his fist onto the hood, making a second dent.

The driver of the cab, a thin, bearded man wearing a turban, stayed in the driver's seat and stared straight ahead, his hands pale from gripping the steering wheel. By now, the owner of the SUV had circled to the cab driver's door.

"Get out of the car." He yanked at the handle, but the door was locked. The cab driver turned on the ignition. "Get out of the goddamned car, you fucking Arab!"

The cab driver rolled down his window. "You stupid American! Why did you run a red light?"

I ♥ New York grabbed the cab driver by the collar and tried to pull him out of the taxi through the window.

A sickening paralysis overwhelmed Richard as a dissonance of car horns rose. Shouldn't he do something? Call 911? Several people in the surrounding crowd were talking on their cellphones. Surely one of them was calling the police. He turned a sharp right and walked quickly toward Ninth Avenue, taking a few deep breaths to calm the pressure building in his chest. The world had grown so unstable. Everyone was so angry. He was actually shaking! He slowed his pace and tried to reclaim his original thought: yes, his finances.

They'd withstood 9/11. The economy had staggered a little, but it didn't collapse, as so many in the media hinted it might. Richard's portfolio was doing just fine, thank you very much. The co-op was worth a fortune, more than twice what they'd paid for it. They were carrying more debt than he liked with the second mortgage on the country house, but he was sure it would pay off in the long run. It had to. It was true that the balances on the credit cards had gotten a little high, but with interest rates so low, it was practically free money.

This logic made Richard wince a little. It was an unpleasant reminder that there was exposure in his planning. But then, their expenses went down in other areas. There were no more checks to write for college tui–. Here, Richard's train of thought hit a bump, and he quickly veered away. *Don't go there. There's nothing to be gained by it.*

Ahead, Lincoln Center shimmered against the backdrop of the night sky. Taxicabs lined the ramp in front of the plaza. Who was he kidding, he thought as he watched a tuxedoed gentleman hand his elegant date into a limo. He and Anna had not lived a life of wealth. It had the appearance of wealth, but it was not real wealth. They had the two-bedroom co-op on the Upper West Side, a car, private schooling for Ben, braces, summer camp, yet Richard had never considered himself well off. Certainly not compared to the parents of Ben's classmates. They made such a big show of spending tens of thousands of dollars at the annual school auction or flying off to St. Bart's over spring break as if all they had to do was cough into their hands and money would appear.

Richard paused in front of a bank to catch his breath. The bulk of his form, dimly reflected in the plate glass window, startled him. How he'd aged over the last year! He looked like a man who had succumbed to gravity with his rounded shoulders, jowly cheeks, and flat, thin hair streaked with gray. Was this how sixty was supposed to look? He straightened his back and resumed his walk at a slower pace.

The force of his whole life was behind him, pushing him toward that dark apartment, toward the diminishing time left to him. Maybe that's why he'd bought the country house. He needed something to look forward to. He knew it was an extravagance. He knew he might have overreached a bit, but he'd been clever. Wily, even. He would never dream of saying it out loud, but thanks to the dip in the housing market, back taxes and death, thanks, in other words, to the misfortunes of others he'd been able to get the house for a song. The sellers had scooped it up from the old man who'd built it. They'd had visions of renovating and flipping it, but when a serious illness struck one of them—cancer, if Richard remembered correctly—they had to sell fast if they were going to avoid bankruptcy.

Meanwhile, the house remained untouched. And how he loved it, its authenticity. He wouldn't change a thing, not the pine walls or the taxidermy, not the linoleum floor in the kitchen, nothing. He was reluctant even to change the furnishings that the sellers had been grateful to leave behind. That house would provide the healing balm that would bring Anna and him back together. They would take walks under a canopy of autumn leaves, read in front of a fire on a snowbound winter's night, laugh with weekend guests around a candlelit dinner table. The house offered them a fresh start. Though rich with its own history, it was not *their* history.

When Broadway met Amsterdam, he stopped, forcing the flow of pedestrians to divert around him while he debated whether to hop in a cab or walk the rest of the way home. Tomorrow was going to be a big day. Maybe it would be best to get home sooner, order takeout, call Anna, and go to bed. A sudden aversion to the quiet hollowness of the apartment swept over him, the loneliness of it. Here on the street, nightlife swirled around him as friends greeted one another with laughter and crowded into busy restaurants.

There was a pulse to the action here, and Richard felt his own heart straining to keep up with it.

Suddenly, he was jostled from behind. He reached for his wallet instinctively as a small band of carousers, twenty-somethings whooping it up and walking with their arms linked, descended upon him. One of them, a short, plump, dark-haired girl slipped her arm through his and pulled him along in their northbound march up Amsterdam Avenue. "No, really," he protested when he realized what was happening.

"Dude. C'mon." A boy on his left, shaggy-headed and reeking of pot took his other arm and leaned in. "You're slowing things down, man." Another girl, a rangy redhead with big teeth and kohl-smudged eyes, cackled.

Richard feigned nonchalance as he pulled his arms free. "Honestly. Thanks anyway, but –"

"Hey!" The dark-hair girl stopped short and stared at him. "I know you."

Richard searched her face. "I can't imagine where –"

"Yeah, yeah. At GFF. Gross Fake Foods or whatever it's called."

"Global Fragrances and Flavors?"

"Yeah, that's it. I've been temping there. I'm filling in for—what's-her-name—Allan's secretary."

Richard took in her disheveled black hair with hot pink streaks running through it and the glittering studs and rings that pierced her ears, nostrils, and lips. "I don't recall..."

"Yeah, you do. I made that crack about, you know, how photocopying causes cancer. And I told Allan he had to stop using the word "flavorist" because it creeps me out. You thought I was funny. I remember."

"Oh? Oh! Jeannie, is it?"

"Gina."

"You look so...different."

She ran her fingers through the mess on her head. "I wear a wig. See?" She reached into a bicycle messenger's bag slung across her chest and pulled out a handful of brown fur. "Sorta looks like roadkill now, but..." she pulled it on, tucking her real hair under it and fluffed the synthetic locks with her fingers. "Et, voila! Miss Priss. Of course, I take out all the hardware," she added, fluttering her fingers in front of her piercings. She leaned in, confiding a great secret. "Corporate America isn't ready yet," then loudly, with a fist thrust skyward, "BUT COME THE REVOLUTION!"

Richard glanced at the other two. They had drifted to the curb to light their cigarettes and were no more interested in him than they were in the street sign they leaned against. The redhead's eyes darted in their direction with a flicker of annoyance.

"Well, uh, Gina, it is very nice to see you again." He put out his hand, which she clasped and held.

"Don't go yet."

"Why wouldn't I?"

"Come have a drink with us. I'll buy you one, and you can buy us a round."

So that was it. "No, really. I've got to go –"

"Oh. Plans, huh?" She actually looked crestfallen.

"No, it's not that, it's just –"

"Then why the hell not?" She gripped his hand more firmly. "Please. Listen, I know we're not your usual crowd, but I would really, *really* like it if you would hang out with us for a little while." She shrugged her shoulders and said in a lighter tone, "I mean, c'mon. How often do you get an invitation from the kids?" She flashed an impish grin. "You never know. You might learn something."

When Richard looked back at that night, he tried in vain to

reconstruct it into a clear narrative. Instead, it came to him in disparate flashes. It started out simply enough with a pitcher of beer at a neighborhood Irish pub. Richard remembered it from the old days before he'd met Anna. A good place to meet friends for cheap beer and salted peanuts, which often amounted to supper back then. It hadn't changed much, although the peanuts had been replaced by the more cost-effective Goldfish, a comedown in Richard's opinion. There was still sawdust on the floor and a jukebox in the back. Odd that it wasn't very crowded; he remembered it as always jam-packed, standing room only.

Richard sat next to Gina in a booth. The boy, Nat sat across from him and stared at the Naugahyde upholstery behind Richard's head. The redhead—Lexi, was it?—slid in next to Nat, dipped her fingers into the bowl of Goldfish, and chucked them one at a time at Gina.

"Cut it out, Lexi." Gina swatted the air in front of her.

"Beer," Lexi chanted, flicking more Goldfish across the table. "Beer. Beer. Beer. I. Want. Beer."

"Fine!" Gina bolted from the booth and headed for the bar.

Lexi swept the loose Goldfish on the table into her palm and popped them into her mouth, eyeballing Richard. A tinny melody emitted from her jacket pocket. She pulled out a cellphone and pressed it to her ear. "Hey, babe! What's up?" She nodded and cackled loudly, turning away from Richard and the boy. It wasn't until Gina reappeared with a pitcher of beer and some glasses that Lexi said, "Later," and quickly pocketed the phone. "Finally!" She grabbed the pitcher and pretended to drink from it directly. "Just kidding." She poured beer into each glass, tipping it slightly, her pinky extended. "Must mind my manners with Daddy here." She passed the glasses around, downed hers in a series of gulps, released a resounding belch, and poured herself another. Then she proceeded to talk, talk, talk.

Gina was the only one of the three who registered Richard's presence. She tried to translate the patter: "Lexi got this new tattoo down in the East Village, some really cool proverb in Chinese, and then found out the guy totally screwed up the characters." Or, "There was this rave in Brooklyn that we heard about, but it took us forever to find the place. We got lost about a million times and saw this really gross..." And so on. At one point, he leaned into Gina.

"I really shouldn't stay long. I've got that thing tomorrow, you know. Need a good night's sleep."

"You haven't finished your beer."

He knew he was being played for booze money, but he was touched by Gina's efforts to get him to stay. There was something about her. Maybe it was just that she was not quite as self-absorbed as so many young people seemed to be. And there was something else. Despite her appearance, she exuded a kind of competence. He appreciated competence.

He remembered her from the office very clearly now. On her first day Allan had muttered a few snide remarks about how some young women in New York seem to go out of their way to look like hell. "My wife won't have to worry about *this* one," he snickered.

It was true that Gina stuck out in her approximation of office attire, even with the wig and without the piercings, but she had saved Allan's ass more than once, correcting the names on correspondence or chasing down his cab to hand him his laptop for a presentation to a client. And that was after only a few days on the job.

"Okay. Just a little longer."

Gina patted his arm and settled into her seat with a contented sigh.

"Hey." The boy, Nat, nodded his head at Richard.

He'd been so quiet; Richard had almost forgotten he was there. He nodded back. "Hey, yourself."

"What is it you do again? Gina tried to explain it to me, but I couldn't figure it out."

Lexi sighed loudly, slid out of the booth, and wandered over to the jukebox. Gina followed her.

"Well, my official title is Chief Flavor Strategist."

"Chief 'Who'?"

"It's hard to explain. Okay. What did you have for lunch today?"

"Sushi."

"Good. Sushi is easy. Anything you eat, any natural food, has flavor, right? And that flavor comes from the food itself. But for the foods I work with, like your sushi, there's something else, some enhancers that give the food an edge and make it taste and smell and feel even more like itself. Or more like what it's supposed to be."

Nat stared at him as if he were trying to see through a block of wood. Richard leaned forward and tried again. "Was your sushi expensive?"

"Eight bucks."

"Pretty good deal."

"Yeah, I guess."

"Did it have crab in it?"

"Yeah. California rolls."

"Well, chances are, you weren't eating real crab, but surimi."

"What the hell is that?"

"It's basically processed pollock mixed in a slurry of starch and oil and salt. It doesn't look or taste at all like crab. That's where I come in. I work with a team that develops colors, textures, scents, and flavors that make that surimi look, feel, smell, and taste like crab."

Nat shook his head. "Why can't I just have crab? Why are you fucking with my food?"

"Because pollock is cheap. Crab isn't. You want sushi for eight bucks, you eat pollock for crab."

"That sucks."

"That, my friend, is life."

It was the same response he had gotten from his own son. One little illusion shattered and the whole world sucks. Never mind that these illusions had paid for a very cushy life, all told. And here it was again, paying for this nitwit's beer.

He didn't like it that this twit, this zonked-out youth reminded him of his dead son. Over the past year, he had made—with some success—a real effort to remember Ben in the best light. He had selected a few gems, a few gleaming memories that he polished and refined until he was able to convince himself that Ben had indeed been the son he had always wanted; the son he deserved. An outing to a dog run in Riverside Park, where seven-year-old Ben sat with him on a bench and listed the various breeds dashing around the dusty corral. Or a college visit to a school in Boston where Ben discussed Scorsese and Coppola with the head of the film department, surprising Richard with the depth of his knowledge.

Richard told himself that if Ben had had the time to develop into a fully formed adult, they might have at last found their stride with each other. In this rendering, Ben would have felt completely comfortable calling Richard out of the blue, "Hey, Dad, I need your advice on something. Can we get together for lunch on Thursday?"

But this boy, this Nat, brought back the image of a sullen, teenaged Ben at the dinner table, slumped over his food, his hair hanging over his face as he pushed the poached salmon around his plate with his fork. Richard couldn't even tell him to sit up, get his elbows off the table, and put his napkin in his lap without inviting a withering glance followed by a sarcastic remark. Not that Anna was any help. The minute the words were out of Richard's mouth, she stiffened and stared grimly at her wine. She should have backed him up, shown Ben that his parents were a united front. Instead, she remained silent. Later she would talk. Boy, would she! When they were alone in their room getting ready for bed, Richard would hear for the umpteenth time that he should be gentler with Ben, that he was going through a rough time at school, that he was *sensitive*.

A pile of misery. That's what Richard saw in Ben. He'd even said it to him once, just before Ben slammed his bedroom door shut. Perhaps that's why the empty apartment gave Richard the willies. All around the place were photographs of Ben and Anna, Anna and Ben, which, yes, Richard had taken when Ben was a child, a rare weekend jaunt to Rye Playland or the Bronx Zoo. Ben with Anna hugging at Camp Getaway on Parents' Day; Anna and Ben at his high school graduation, both clutching his diploma and grinning at the camera. Richard had been able to capture the joy that passed between them, but he remained untouched by it. Theirs was a life that existed alongside his own, a parallel universe that he could witness but not enter. So, he accepted the lesser role of documentarian.

Richard glanced over at Gina, who had her arm draped around Lexi's waist and was bumping her with her hip to the beat of the tune playing on the jukebox. Lexi turned away and walked back to the table with a flirty little swagger, her eyes darting between Nat and Richard.

"I'm bored."

Nat slid toward the wall and patted the bench next to him. With a giggle, she slipped in and licked his ear, ignoring Richard's presence. He stood and walked over to Gina at the jukebox.

She was studying the song titles with great interest, but when Richard drew close, she stiffened and wiped her nose on her sleeve. He put his hand on her shoulder. "You okay?"

She smiled ruefully at him and nodded. Her eyes were red, the black liner surrounding them had smeared. "Here." He reached into his pocket and pulled out a handkerchief.

She laughed.

"What?"

"You're the only guy I know who goes around with an actual handkerchief in his pocket."

"It's a generational thing. I'll bet your dad has one in his pocket."

"Not a chance. Maybe a wad of steel wool." She took the handkerchief and wiped her eyes.

Richard scanned the songs in the jukebox. He didn't recognize many of the artists. Van Morrison, of course. He was a keeper. Old Frank Sinatra doing that tune with his daughter, *Something Stupid*. Who the hell was Gnarls Barkley? "I remember when these were all vinyl 45's," he said more to himself than to Gina. "Now it's all CDs, and even those are outdated. Wonder what it'll be in another ten years."

Gina didn't answer. She had turned her back to the jukebox and was staring at Lexi and Nat. They sat with their heads together, laughing at some idiocy, while Lexi swirled Richard's glass of half-consumed beer. Gina's eyes were wide open, almost childlike. A sudden wave of tenderness swept over Richard as he spied a glimmer of what it might have been like to have a daughter. "Don't worry about him," he said, nodding toward Nat. "He's not worth it."

"Huh?"

"You can do a lot better than him."

Gina turned slowly and stared at him. Then she smiled and patted his cheek. "You old fool. What you see and don't see."

They returned to the table for a quick conference. Lexi insisted they check out a club downtown. Gina tugged at Richard's sleeve. "C'mon," she begged. "It'll be fun."

Fun. Something he hadn't had in a long time. The specter of the empty apartment faded as Richard slugged down the remains of his beer, which had grown slightly bitter as it warmed, paid the tab and followed them out the door.

Spurred by Lexi's sudden burst of enthusiasm, they raced down the block and crossed 72nd Street. Richard struggled to keep up. When they dodged oncoming traffic on Broadway to get to the subway station on the mall, the blare of a horn and screaming brakes brought him up short. A cab driver leaned out his window, yelling. Richard smiled an apology, then noticed a familiar face staring at him through the backseat window. Could that be Allan? He raised his hand to wave, but Gina grabbed his arm. "C'mon! I hear a train!"

She pulled him into the belly of the city. *Or more like the intestines,* he thought to himself with a giggle. He hadn't ridden the subway in years, preferring the relative cleanliness of buses and cabs. Yes, they were slower, but he had reached an age at which safety mattered more than speed.

And speed there was. They chose the first car on the express, and Gina let him have the best spot: the front window. He was a boy again, Superman, hurtling down the tracks, taking the twists and turns without a hitch, zipping past local stops, flashing through light, dark, light, dark, as if he were traveling through time itself.

When they came out at the other end, they were in a place he didn't recognize, a new wonderland that hummed with traffic and young people, so many young people dressed in black, black, black. The street pulsed with them. Gina took him by the hand and led him through the crowd, weaving in and out and around through cigarette smoke and weed smoke, through a stench of coffee, booze, urine, and garbage. Finally, with a sharp swerve to the right, Gina pulled him into a dark doorway and followed Lexi and Nat up a narrow flight of stairs that opened onto a loft flashing with light.

The air was smokey and stale and throbbed with music, metallic and insistent. Video walls played Japanese cartoons, while large spots of colored light roamed the floor, creating a vertiginous effect. Richard followed the others to a cluster of tattered loveseats surrounding two postage stamp-sized tables. He squeezed into a spot next to Gina, glad to be off his feet. His head felt light and his throat dry.

The room tilted precariously. He shut his eyes to make it stop. When he opened them again, he wondered if they hadn't stumbled into some kind of costume party. On a round dais in the center of the room two women in satin party dresses ate fire. The dance floor around them was filled with men in skintight jeans and work shirts and women in underwear: bustiers, panties, garter belts, fishnet stockings, and stiletto heels. They swayed and gyrated, slowly swinging their bottoms from side to side as they lowered themselves to the floor. Richard watched a nearby couple merge in one serpentine movement and join at the mouth, while the two fire-eaters dipped long vibe-sticks into jars of something, kissed their tips, and blew flames into the air. "It's all women here. Even the men are women." Richard heard his own voice as if it had left his body, traveled the room, and returned with a report. He turned to Gina, but she was deep into a heated conversation with Nat and Lexi. With limbs of lead, he was anchored to his seat. If the room caught fire, he wouldn't be able to move.

"You're not in Kansas anymore, sweetie."

Richard turned to his left and saw a man—*no, a woman,* he thought—with shorty-short hair, wearing a three-piece business suit. On her neck below her ear was a tattoo of a price code. A dollar bill covered her mouth. It took a tremendous effort to work his tongue. "Did you say something?" The suit looked at him with doleful eyes and left him for the dance floor. "How can you talk with that money on your mouth?" he called.

It was so hot. Sweat trickled down his face. The collar of his shirt squeezed his throat. He wanted to go to sleep. He wrestled his tie loose and struggled to free himself from his sports jacket. He turned to Gina for help, but she was still arguing with Nat.

"Relax, for fuck's sake, Gina. He's a big boy."

"You had no right –"

"*He* has no right. This is just a little payback. He screws with my food; I screw with his beer."

Richard leaned in, still tangled in his jacket. "You screwed my beer?" he asked with the simple innocence of a child.

"I want some! I want some!" Lexi bounced in her seat.

Gina banged her hand on the table and pointed a ferocious finger at Lexi. "No! You promised."

"Did you screw this, too?" Richard picked up one of the drinks that had miraculously materialized on the table.

Nat laughed. "See? He's not feeling any pain."

"I'm not so good at promises," Lexi deadpanned. She snaked her hand into Nat's crotch. "C'mon, Nat. Let's dance." She led him onto the floor, where Nat stood, merely swaying. Lexi grabbed him by the belt, pulled him to her, and wrapped one leg around his hips.

"Wow," Richard said. "She's got great balance."

Gina glared at her. "Fucking show-off."

Lexi smiled back and unwrapped her leg. "Bye, Mommy," she waved as she pulled Nat deeper into the crowd.

Richard laid his head on Gina's shoulder. "I don't feel so good."

She sighed and took his face in her hands. "Let me look at you. No, don't collapse on me. And wipe that stupid grin off your face. This is serious. Open your eyes. *Open them.*"

"I'm trying."

She held up his jacket, his arm still trapped in one sleeve. "What's this?"

"I'm hot."

She peeled it off and draped it over Richard's arm. "Don't lose it."

"Yes, ma'am."

"We better get you some water."

Once again, he followed her through the sweat and din of the crowd. Bodies bumped against him as he teetered after her. Gina took his hand and led him to a hallway near the stairs. Suddenly, the noise dropped away. It was dark there, so dark. He could fall asleep in a nice dark place like this. Gina slung his arm around her shoulders and held him up around the waist. "C'mon, the restroom is just a little farther."

Richard felt his stomach rise to his throat, and an alarming tang filled his mouth. "I think I'm going to be sick."

"You can make it."

Richard fixed his eyes on the door, several feet away. There was an odd shape just beyond it, a giraffe, it seemed, or maybe a large chair, but alive, its seat moving up and down.

"Goddammit!" Suddenly, Gina's arms dropped away from him, and he staggered against the wall. "Motherfucker!" She was beating the giraffe, the chair. She pulled it apart, slapping the giraffe, slapping the chair.

"Fuck you, Gina!" The chair—Lexi—rose from her knees and pushed Gina back. The giraffe zipped his fly and slid past them toward the stairs. Lexi followed him.

"Nat! Come back! You owe me something!"

"Come on, Lex, don't do it." Gina clutched Lexi's arm, but Lexi shook her off and turned on her, all eyes and teeth.

"I don't want you! Don't you get it? I don't want any part of your fat, pathetic, mommy ass!" She turned and ran down the stairs after Nat.

Gina managed a quick glance in Richard's direction. "I'll be right back," she said before she followed Lexi.

Richard slid down the wall to his knees. His mouth filled with acid that he emptied onto the floor again and again. It splashed down his shirt, pants, and onto his jacket. He seemed to be losing liquid everywhere. When it was over at last, he closed his eyes and rested his cheek against the blessedly cool wall. He was vaguely aware that he was sitting in a pool of everything that had passed through his stomach over the last few hours, but he didn't move. He would wait. He would wait so he would be right there when Gina came back.

Friday

3

A shaft of morning sunlight cut across Anna's pillow. She turned her head and threw her arm over her face. She hadn't slept, really. Sleep still came in small doses, though for longer stretches lately.

There was still that moment after she woke when she forgot and then remembered that life had taken a turn. Then she indulged in the torturous fantasy that by replaying the events of a year ago, she could restore Ben to life. In her revisions, Ben and his killer never meet. Or if they meet, the man is content simply to shove Ben against the wall, take his wallet and be done with it. Sometimes Ben's hand brushes the barrel of the gun aside, placing him miraculous millimeters out of death's reach. Sometimes even, it is someone else who dies. The mugger. A passing stranger. Someone else's son. These thoughts pressed into her, made her head throb and her body ache. If she devoted herself to them too ardently, they could keep her in bed for days.

Anna rolled over and tried to think of something else. Her mind hit on the weekend when Richard and she drove to Philadelphia to clean out Ben's apartment. It was a mess, of course. Ben had always been a terrible slob. The bed was a snarl of dingy sheets. Food-crusted dishes filled the sink. Clothes were strewn about the floor like molted skins.

Richard set to work at the desk while Anna picked up a hooded sweatshirt hanging from the back of a chair. She ran her fingers over it, held it to her nose, searching for warmth, for musk, for a trace of the living Ben.

He changed after he left for college. With each visit, he brought home surprises: a tattoo of the word *"fly"* on his wrist, a silver ring pierced through the cartilage of his ear and another at the edge of his eyebrow. She hadn't been shocked or concerned; this was what kids do these days. But she was curious. She, who had known this boy all his life, wondered what these markings could tell her about the person he was becoming. When he was a child, the odds and ends she routinely fished out of his pockets provided a glimpse of his life away from her: rocks, sticks, and Legos when he was younger; gum wrappers or a computer thumb drive when he was in high school. After he left home for college, he guarded his privacy with a firmness that surprised her. When he came home for Thanksgiving during his freshman year, she noticed his piercings. "Do you need any hydrogen peroxide for cleaning the holes?"

Ben held up his hand. "Mom? Mom. Relax."

Richard had been no help at all. "Let the boy, alone, for God's sake. Cut the apron strings."

"You always say that."

"Well, I mean, what are you going to do? Move in with him? Cut his meat for him?"

"Don't be ridiculous."

"It's about time he learned to cut his own meat. Right, Ben?"

"I'm a vegetarian, Dad."

That day in Ben's apartment, as she sorted through personal belongings that he never thought his mother would see: a stash of weed inside an old Altoids tin, photographs he'd taken of police clearing homeless people from Rittenhouse Square, a couple of message buttons: *Straight, But Not Narrow; Who Would Jesus Bomb?* Anna realized that this was it, the end of a lifetime's trail of clues. She would never have more than this odd collection of artifacts to touch, to run her fingertips over in her search for the meaning of Ben's life.

She didn't speak to Richard of these discoveries. He would be in favor of tossing the lot. Instead, she tucked them into a shoebox. When Richard noticed, he didn't argue. He simply shook his head—"Suit yourself."—and returned his attention to Ben's unpaid bills.

The shoebox was with her now. She had brought it along with a second, simple box made of sturdy cardboard with the logo of a funeral home stamped on the lid. Inside was a plastic bag filled with Ben's ashes, closed with an ordinary green twist tie, the kind she kept in the corner of a kitchen drawer. They rested, these boxes, side by side on the closet shelf.

In the weeks following Ben's memorial service, Anna and Richard had not been able to agree on what to do with the ashes. Richard's parents were buried in the small upstate town where he'd grown up, and the ashes of Anna's father and mother were scattered in the backyard of her childhood home on Long Island, a house that had been sold years ago.

Richard was in favor of purchasing an urn for Ben's ashes and putting it in a columbarium at some place up in Westchester called Cedar Rest. "No," Anna objected when he first presented the idea.

"Why not?"

"That place has nothing to do with us."

"Well, I don't know what you want. We can't exactly throw him under a bush in Riverside Park. There's probably a law against it, first of all. And he'd just get peed on by dogs or get mixed up with rat poison and litter."

"Are you making a joke out of this?"

"Anna, I'm just pointing out the realities. We don't have any land of our own, and none of the public land that meant anything to Ben—Riverside Park, Central Park—is suitable. Cedar

Rest makes sense. It's close by; it's clean and dignified. I just think it would be nice to have it settled. While I'm at it, I could make arrangements for us, as well."

"What? Why? Richard—" Anna put her hand on his arm and spoke in a softer tone. "Who is going to visit us? We have no family now. There will be no grandchildren, no descendants at all. Don't you understand? You and I are the end of the line."

"I—"

"Please. Stop. Just stop. Stop trying to wrap everything up and put it away. We don't have to decide anything now. Let's just...hold onto him a little longer." Here, her voice caught and left off. He had not raised the issue since.

But now they did own land, just a little. Perhaps here they would find a place for Ben.

The heat of the electric blanket made Anna thirsty. She glanced at the nightstand next to the bed and wished she'd set out a glass of water the night before. It was no use. In a minute she would have to get up. She flicked on the clock radio next to the bed, a habit of hers since 9/11. Check the news. Make sure the world was still there, that the city, as she knew it, was still there.

After a brief rundown of the day's stories—starvation and slaughter in Africa, the Middle East on fire, another mass shooting at a shopping mall in the Midwest—there was a musical interlude, lilting and familiar, then a hand-off to the local affiliate who told her that temperatures would rise to unseasonable highs, the sun would shine, then give way to clouds. Rain, heavy at times, possible thunderstorms with gusting winds. *Something for everyone*, she thought as she turned off the radio and got out of bed.

The thermostat in the hall read 49 degrees. She stared at it for a moment, as if the numbers didn't make sense and turned it up to 55. Richard liked to keep a cold house.

A machine fired up outside. An engine. She ducked back into the bedroom, grabbed her robe and ran to the living room. Through a window she saw a red pickup truck with a flatbed trailer in the driveway. On the side lawn, a man was driving a tractor on the grass.

He pulled a bladed attachment across the sod, leaving behind a swath of upturned soil. After twenty feet, he turned left and cut another path. Anna stepped into a pair of rubber boots next to the front door and went out to the porch. "What are you doing?" she called.

He didn't hear her. She scuttled down the steps, crossed the lawn with her arms folded, and circled to the front of the tractor where he could see her. "What are you doing?"

He cut off the engine.

He was not a man. He was a boy, maybe eighteen or nineteen. He curved over the steering wheel as if he had been fitted to it and straightened only slightly when he saw her. "What are you doing?" she repeated.

The boy ducked his head, looked back at the path he'd cut, then turned back to her. "He said you wanted a garden."

"Yes, but I thought I'd cut it myself." She knew who he was.

"With what?"

He was the caretaker's son. "I have a shovel."

The boy snorted and turned his face away from her. "Well. I can't put it back."

Anna looked at the patch. Clods of earth the size of her head lay in a jumble. They would still need to be chopped up to make good topsoil. *Cultivating,* she thought it was called. "No. Of course you can't."

He straightened completely and stretched as he looked toward the old apple orchard beyond the lawn. He was long-limbed with big wrists and hands. A tangle of dark hair poked from under the bill of his cap. Beneath that she could see he had fine features, dark eyes, and a faint scatter of acne scars on his cheeks. He rubbed his hand along his opposite forearm, then sagged and became ancient. An old timer rubbing a war wound. The boy tugged the cuff of his sleeve over his wrist. "So, you want me to stop?"

She did and she didn't. He had already cut a good bit of the plot. It seemed ridiculous to stop him now. But she had looked forward to breaking the earth herself. She had wanted the garden to be hers from start to finish. Richard must have arranged this. His thoughtfulness irritated her.

How she must look to this boy, lumpy in her bathrobe and rubber boots. Hair shot with gray and still wild from sleep. Complaining when he was doing her a kindness. "No. You might as well finish." Anna started back to the house, then stopped and turned. "Thank you," she remembered.

In the kitchen, she put the kettle on for coffee. Outside, the tractor's engine droned.

So, this was spring in the country. It wasn't just the return of flowers, birds, and insects. It was the return of machines, the constant hum of tractors and chainsaws and lawnmowers.

Spring in the city was intoxicating and short-lived. It was years since Anna made it to Central Park in time to catch the lilacs in bloom. She first saw them when she was a young woman, newly married, starting graduate studies at Columbia, and as she had just learned an hour earlier in her doctor's office, pregnant.

She was walking across the park to Richard's and her apartment with her head down, deep in thought. A baby. Her future rushed toward her as if she had turned a corner and come up against a brick wall. She would hold on for as long as possible, but she knew that her studies would grind to a halt. Money would become even tighter. She would have to find some kind of work until the baby came. They would outgrow their tiny apartment. Richard would worry. Everything would change.

Another thought flickered at the periphery of her mind. She could not bear to look at it directly, yet the more she avoided it, the more it stared her down.

Toby.

It was ludicrous.

That one sad fuck?

How could anything so pathetic have the power to create life?

That bitter weekend in January.

She'd gone home to visit her mother and make her annual pilgrimage to the site of her father's death, a scrubby bend in a road on the outskirts of town. The ancient hickory tree had survived the impact of her father's pickup, absorbing the abuse as it had absorbed all the other abuses of its long, tired history. She stood in a snowdrift and rested her gloved hand on the tree trunk. She imagined the shower of shattered windshield glass ricocheting off the scaly bark. An instant later, her father's body—a rage-flung toy—slammed into the tree. Then an awful stillness.

She wasn't sure what she hoped to find on these yearly pilgrimages. The hollowness inside her never closed. If anything, it opened wider, demanding to be fed. Later, when she ran into Toby in the village and he invited her to come by his restaurant for a nightcap, she caved, even though she knew exactly what to expect.

It was well after closing time when she showed up. The crew had gone home, and the back door was unlocked, as she knew it would be. His welcome mat. As she stepped into the dark kitchen and walked past the prep station and a collection of pots dangling from an overhead rack, Anna was struck by the familiarity of the trek. Toby was in his office, as usual, closing out the books for the night.

"'Bout time you got here," he said, not looking up.

"I almost didn't come."

He closed the ledger and leaned back in his chair. "Bullshit."

She lingered in the doorway. *Jesus, they were fighting already.* "So, how's business? Richard will want to know."

Toby laughed. "Yes, he will. It's okay. Slow this time of year, but we'll scrape by. I had to lay off most of the waitstaff for the season, but I still have Sherry."

"Sherry? Really?"

Toby raised an eyebrow. "Why so surprised?"

"I don't know. It's just..." The shelf life of Toby's dalliances with his summer hires usually expired in the fall when the girls either returned to school or Toby cut their schedules down to a string. Anna knew how it worked all too well.

"Now, now. She's the *breast* waitress I've got."

"Ah, yes. Well, there's that."

Toby led her out to the house and pulled a couple of beers from behind the bar. Then he dropped some quarters into the jukebox, punched in a Marvin Gaye song—way too obvious—lit up a joint and handed it to her. "Sherry's okay. She gets me. Doesn't expect anything. We've got this kind of 'open thing' going."

"Wow." Anna inhaled and held the smoke in her lungs. She loved the first hit, the way its wispy fingers spread through her chest, clenched her lungs, then trailed up to her head and massaged her mind. It had been a while; Richard disapproved. She swayed slightly to Marvin's sultry suggestions. "Works out nicely for you," she exhaled.

Toby sat on the bar stool next to her and squeezed her knee. "C'mon. Be nice." He let his hand rest there. "She's not like you. No one is like you."

Anna laughed and handed him the joint. "That comment leaves a lot of room for interpretation."

"No, I mean it. I'll admit, I was jealous when Richard came and swept you up."

"He didn't exactly 'sweep me up.'"

"Turned you away from me."

"You and I had moved on by then."

"I'm not sure I really had. Not really. I think maybe I was just scared."

"You? C'mon. Of what?"

Toby took a pull on his beer and draped his arm along the back of her stool. "Of getting in too deep. You might have been the one that got away, Anna."

She patted his cheek with her hand. "You amaze me. You will say anything to get laid."

Toby turned his head and kissed her palm. Then he stood and pressed himself against her legs, forcing them apart. "Why not, if it gets me what I want?" He leaned into her and ran his lips along her neck.

"Toby, I don't know about this. Richard—"

"Screw Richard. I saw you first." His thumb strummed her nipple as he silenced her with his mouth. Her hunger woke, ravenous and alert, the hollowness within her cracked wide open. She answered his lips, his tongue, his heat, not sure if she was making love to him or to the hunger. Toby had a slow, sure hand guided by intent. He was not at all like Richard who was tender and concerned, who fumbled and apologized in bed. Lit with fever, Anna unzipped Toby's pants and pushed him back into his seat. He peeled her sweater over her head, pulled her onto his lap, and entered her in one motion. As she ground herself against him, her hunger closed around him. She tried to pull all of him inside her, fill the gaping cavity and take her back to a young, twitchy past when desire and fun were all that mattered, a time of innocence and infinite possibilities.

Afterward, they returned to their respective barstools and turned slightly away from each other. Anna watched Toby in the mirror behind the bar as he relit the joint, took a hit, and handed it to her.

"So, it's good with Richard?" When she didn't answer, he continued. "He's a good guy. You could do worse."

"I think I just did."

"What?"

She turned to him, leaning an elbow on the bar. "You really don't care about me at all, do you?"

"Of course I do. I think you're great." He took another hit. "I lost a great piece of ass when you two got married."

"Jesus. I'm such an idiot."

"What did you think—I was going to wreck your marriage? Richard's one of my best buds. I wouldn't do that."

Anna slid off the stool and searched for her sweater. "Yeah. You're a real stand-up guy."

"Hey, no need to be insulting. Don't forget, you came to see *me*."

Anna gathered her jacket and purse. "Yes, I did." She shook her head. "I guess I'm just a slow learner."

When she got back to the city the next day, she barely set down her bags before she stripped off Richard's shirt and hauled him into bed. It was a kind of apology, this repentant lovemaking. When he noticed her crying afterwards, she hoped he simply took it as a testament of how much she'd missed him.

As Anna turned onto the promenade in Central Park, she did a quick calculation in her head and realized it was possible.

Unlikely, but... She slowed her pace. Would this be a secret that she would carry to her grave? A constant question? Richard's or Toby's child? She knew one thing: the child was hers. To that certainty she would hold tight.

Suddenly, the path turned and there they were: lilac bushes clustered like ladies at a garden party. They swayed in the breeze, their leaves fluttering to reveal their pale undersides. She stopped and rested her hand on what she imagined was a swell in her abdomen. A delicate fragrance wove in and out of the green, violet, and mauve. She drew it in deeply, invited it to thread its way into her pores. She carried it home with her and could swear that even in the living room of their small, flowerless apartment, she could still smell lilacs.

A few years later she returned with Ben, curious if, at the age of two and a half, he, too, would fall under the spell of the lilac grove. He bypassed it entirely, however, in favor of an Olympic-sized puddle on the promenade. He stood on its edge and tossed pebble after pebble into the water. "I make ravioli," he explained.

Anna watched him toddle to the path and squat to grab more stones, his corduroy jacket bunching under his chin. He carried the pebbles back to the puddle's edge and hurled them in a shallow arc. A chorus of staccato *plunks,* then silent ripples radiated in concentric circles. Ben turned to Anna and uttered a little scream of delight as he stamped his feet and ran to the path for more pebbles. As Anna sat on the bench, she inhaled deeply, not wanting this moment to end, and caught the faintest whiff of lilacs.

Anna took her coffee to the living room, retrieved a magazine from her bag, and settled into an armchair by the window. As she pulled a throw over her legs, she looked out at the boy, still driving the tractor, then returned to her magazine and opened it to a particular article.

She took a sip of coffee.

Looked out the window again.

Glanced at the words.

Another sip of coffee.

Forced her eyes to scan a line of text.

It was no use.

Once a great pleasure, reading had become one of those things she could no longer do. She could handle simple fare: a recipe in a cookbook or an illustrated sidebar in her gardening magazine that depicted the root system of a carrot. But she could no longer follow the intricacies of a story. And she certainly couldn't manage the complexities of composting in *Organic Gardening Today*.

It was a joke, really. She was supposed to be serious about rebuilding her life—"on the mend," as Richard called it. He was a great believer in the healing power of work. But it was all a farce. A veneer that she polished from time to time to keep him from worrying and pestering her with too many questions. How was she supposed to learn to garden when she couldn't even read? When her mind slipped over words like water over stones?

Anna looked out the window again.

That boy. There was something about that boy. Maybe it was the way he slumped his shoulders and hung his head.

Ben used to hunch like that. It was the posture of loneliness. At a block party years ago, held to raise money for Ben's middle school, Anna watched him as she worked her shift at the bake sale table. He had attached himself to a pack of five or six boys who roamed from booth to booth. They were bent on mischief; Anna could tell that much even from a distance. They swatted one another and sent up loud yelps of ridicule. Sometimes, one of them peeled off from the group to scout a cluster of girls and then loped back to the pack with a snarky comment answered with laughter.

At one point they drew close enough for Anna to hear them mock an old man fingering crocheted scarves at the stand next to hers. When he moved on, they found plenty of other targets, and when there was a lull in passersby, they sniped at one another.

Ben stood at the edge of this group, his hands jammed into the pockets of his jeans. He didn't join in with the taunts. As far as Anna could tell, he didn't say anything. He was all but invisible to them and seemed to prefer it that way. But she also saw how his body leaned toward them like a compass needle straining to find north.

Near the end of that school year, he changed. He took to wearing baggy jeans slung so low they were in constant danger of falling to his ankles. He bobbed around the apartment with earphones fixed to his head, muttering staccato hip-hop lyrics: "*Ain't no mothafucka like me. Uh. Uh-uh-uh. Ain't no mothafucka like me...*" Anna was fascinated by this transformation, but she knew the entirety of his history; this was Ben at his most vulnerable. He clung to this head-bopping persona with the fervor of a recent convert. It gave him someone to be in this uncertain world.

When Ben died, she'd been granted a month off from the Upper East Side private school where she taught English, but in the weeks that followed her return to work, it became clear that she was in no shape to teach. Looking back, she supposed her students and colleagues were trying to be sympathetic. At the time, however, they seemed shockingly dense. She found herself snapping at students when she had to repeat herself because they hadn't been listening in the first place. She no longer bothered to conceal her impatience when discussions at faculty meetings veered hopelessly off-topic.

And, of course, there was the incident with the Salter boy, whose father (as she was constantly reminded by the head of her department) was a major donor to the Annual Fund. The boy was a popular slacker with a gift for ridicule that he employed with glee to keep outcasts relegated to the fringes of the social landscape. In class, he sat in the back and talked to his friends or nodded off. He handed in homework sporadically. When he did turn in assignments, they were either of dreadful quality or clearly not his own work. She tried to reach him, to draw him out during discussions or pull him aside after class to offer extra help, but he just stared at her as if she were asking him to drink bile.

Secretly, she detested him.

One afternoon a few weeks after her return to work, she was at her desk, trying to keep a headache at bay as she wrote a final exam.

"Mrs. Scofield." He was leaning in the doorway, his head bobbing to whatever was coming to him through the wires that snaked up to his ears.

"Yes, Ian."

"What's up with that grade you gave me on that paper?"

"You mean your term paper?"

"Yeah, that one."

"The one that was late?"

He pulled out the ear jacks and let them dangle over his shoulders. They leaked a deep, percussive rhythm. Her headache had gained ground and was settling in between her eyes. "Wasn't my fault," he said. "My stupid tutor was out of town for some family thing."

"You didn't follow the guidelines. You turned in a sloppy, handwritten draft that showed no grasp of the subject, there was no thesis, no bibliography, and you never turned in your notes."

"Stupid cleaning lady threw them out when she cleaned my room."

"You could have talked to me ahead of time, let me know you

were having trouble –"

"Besides, with you out and all, you never really said when it was due."

"Yes, I did. It was written on the board and on the guidelines that I gave you; I must have mentioned it in class at least five times; and it was posted on the webpage."

"Who the fuck looks at the webpage?"

"Ian –"

"It's not my fault."

Anna shook her head and returned to her work.

"My parents aren't going to like this."

"That's not *my* fault."

"Yeah, it is. You screwed up."

"Ian. I'm not changing your grade. You're the one taking this class, not your tutor or your cleaning lady or your parents. And not me. The grade you received is the grade you earned."

"What the fuck!" He gave a little laugh of disbelief. "You're supposed to help me."

"We're finished here."

"My dad pays to have you help me."

Anna rose from her seat and put her hand on his shoulder to steer him toward the door. He jerked away.

"Don't touch me."

"You need to leave. Now."

"Fucking bitch."

Her hand moved faster than her mind. A good, hard smack right across his face. He was taller than she, but she'd managed to get a good purchase; his head jerked to the side, his cheek blazing red. She pointed a finger at his face. "That's *Ms.* Fucking Bitch to you."

His eyes and mouth gaped with shock; for a moment he lost

the ability even to curse. The lower half of his face trembled. *Good,* she thought. *He's going to cry.* Anna smiled at him, questioningly.

He clamped his mouth shut a moment, then: "You are so fired. My dad is so going to kick your *ass* out of this school."

As she watched him run down the hall, she touched her forehead. *How nice,* she thought. *My headache is gone.*

She walked home through Central Park that afternoon, buoyed by an almost overwhelming wave of euphoria. Joggers circled the reservoir, and the cries of children rose like birdsong from a nearby playground. Was this going to be her life from now on? Sudden and wild swings from grief to rage to joy? She knew life would never be the same. She knew what it would *not* be. But she had no idea what it might be. All she knew was that some people, after suffering a great loss, grew kinder, more compassionate and grounded. She did not seem to be one of these people.

The next morning when Anna arrived at work, the secretary told her that the Head of School wanted to see her. Immediately. *Ah, yes,* thought Anna. *The other shoe.*

Sharon Colby was reading her emails when Anna knocked on her door. Without lifting her eyes from her computer, she motioned for Anna to sit in a blue armchair in front of her desk. While she finished attending to her correspondence, Anna gazed at the bookshelves stocked with academic journals, educational trade books, and honorary plaques. Colby's well-polished desk was devoid of clutter, except for a framed photograph of her family: her husband, herself, and Madison, their adopted daughter from Guatemala who, in the third grade, was a notorious tattletale.

From her monogrammed cardigan with grosgrain trim and pearl buttons to the silk scarf she wore to conceal the crepe-like folds of her neck, Colby presented the same quality of restraint as her office. Anna had always found her precision a little unnerving, and now it made her feel like a sloppy, disobedient child called into the principal's office. Finally, Colby lowered the screen of her laptop, removed her reading glasses, and regarded Anna.

"Well, Anna. I hardly know what to say."

Anna said nothing.

"The Salters are understandably quite upset about this incident. I must say that I, too, am shocked and not a little disappointed."

"You do know that Ian was trying to get me to change his grade."

"I understand that he came to you for help."

"No. He came to me to issue a directive, as if I were an extension of his domestic staff. When I refused, he insulted me."

"And you hit him and used profanity."

"Yes."

"A completely inappropriate response."

"At the time it felt...exactly right."

Colby pursed her lips slightly, then reached for a file on her credenza and placed it on the desk between Anna and herself. On the tab was Anna's name. With her fingertips resting on it lightly, she said, "The Salters say they won't sue if you leave."

"What about Ian?"

"Anna. *You* struck *him*. As far as I can tell, the boy was acting within his rights. It is *your* behavior that is in question here, and I, for one –"

"Sharon," Anna interrupted, smiling. "Don't you think there are enough assholes in the world? Do we really want to nurture another one?"

Colby's fingers twitched, and she blinked rapidly for a few moments. Then she folded her hands on top of the file as if to anchor its fate and spoke in the even tones that she used with unruly children. "Anna, I'm concerned about you."

"Why? Because I won't allow a spoiled slacker to call me a fucking bitch?"

"Are you getting help?"

"Are you asking me as a friend or as my soon-to-be-former employer? Because really, Sharon, it seems to me that you are perilously close to violating my right to privacy."

Colby sat back in her chair as if she were bracing herself against a strong wind. "I am merely trying to ascertain –"

"Whether I'm stable? If I'm a suitable role model for a little shit like Salter, who's going to grow up to be a big shit just like his daddy?"

"All right. That's enough."

"My son's death has nothing to do with this. If my son were still alive, Ian Salter still would have come into my office to ask me to change his grade. He still would have insulted me when I refused, and I still would have smacked him upside his head."

"Really, Anna? Would you? That's what I'm asking."

"God, I hope so. It's an ugly job, Sharon, but someone's gotta do it. It will probably be the only thing he'll remember from school."

That night, Anna flushed an entire bottle of antidepressants down the toilet. She didn't want to miss a thing, not a single, searing ribbon of pain that wrapped itself around her heart. This was familiar territory, the land of sorrow. She had come to know it a lifetime of Januarys ago in the wake of her father's death. She and her mother clung to each other back then, sleeping in the same bed, quietly weeping as they boxed up his clothes to give to Goodwill. She knew one thing about the landscape of grief; there was no escaping its borders.

Anna looked out the window. The boy had almost finished cutting the plot. She tried to remember what she had heard about him. The realtor had said something in hushed tones. A rumor.

Some kind of local gossip that ricocheted from the hardware store to the beauty salon to the realtor's office, and so to Anna. At the time, she waved it off as something that had nothing to do with her. These were small, simple lives. They had to contend with farm accidents that took limbs or pinned people under tractors when tree stumps revolted. These were the kind of people who wore metal plates in their heads because of hunting mishaps, or who got struck by lightning and walked around for the rest of their lives with some bizarre gift for divination that proved to be both a blessing and a curse.

Yet now as she watched him hunch over the steering wheel, she wished she had listened to the realtor. She wished she *paid attention*. It was something to do with his arms. Something terrible.

Anna reached for her purse and pulled out a pen and a small pad. She tore out a piece of paper.

I tried to light a fire last night, she wrote, *but it was no good. In all your summers at camp, did you ever learn how to light a fire? Is this another thing I never knew about you?*

The tractor's engine cut off. Anna looked out the window and watched the boy climb down from the seat and stretch.

I met a boy today. He's tall, like you, and has your way of standing as if he wishes he could fade into the scenery. There is great pain there, I think.

I miss you. I miss you. I miss you.

I do.

Anna capped the pen and looked out the window once more. The boy had moved to the other side of the tractor and was blocked from view. She stood and placed the paper and a box of matches on the hearth. Then she went into the bedroom and fetched Ben's ashes from the closet shelf. When she returned to the fireplace, she knelt, lifted the lid from the box, undid the twist tie, and carefully nested the opening of the plastic bag around the ashes. She struck a match and the air filled with the acrid scent of sulfur, a smell she had come to love. When she touched a corner of the note to the flame, the fire advanced quickly, consuming the paper with red-laced blackness that obliterated her words and resigned them to ash.

"There now," Anna murmured as she gently swept the ashes—delicate black petals—into her hand, laid them on top of Ben's ashes and carefully stirred them together with her fingertip. After she secured the plastic bag with the twist tie and closed box back up, she wondered, not for the first time, if the day would ever come when she would take off the lid and find an answer waiting for her, written in Ben's unmistakable scrawl on a slip of paper as ordinary as anything she might find in her desk drawer.

For a year now, she had been searching for a miracle, some blessing buried in the waste of this disaster, a counterbalance to this senseless tragedy, this inversion of a miracle. She was searching for a light to the shadow. But she kept slamming up against the hard truth that Ben was gone. He was never coming back. There was nothing left of him but ashes. The ashes of her longing rested with the ashes of his remains. She could no longer tell them apart.

By the time the boy drove off, the day had warmed up. As Anna walked the perimeter of the garden plot, she realized she would have to work out a plan. Make some sort of map of the garden. She had thumbed through enough gardening books to glean that much. Her mind rolled over and went to sleep when she came to chapters on dirt composition: macro and micronutrients, soil pH. She just wanted to put the damn seeds into the ground, water them every so often, and watch them grow.

Apparently, however, vegetables needed care and attention as much as anything else in this world. And protection. Everything she read, everyone she talked to cautioned her. The world was a hungry place, full of empty stomachs just waiting to feed off her labor. Deer would jump six-foot fences. Woodchucks would tunnel under them and in one night devour everything in sight. Japanese beetles would make lace of her bean leaves just when it was time to harvest.

She was sick to death of these dire warnings. They wanted her to avoid the undertaking altogether. So, she would dig a trench and sink chicken wire a foot underground to block the woodchucks. She would extend the height of the fence to twelve feet to keep the deer out and spray the ground with bottled coyote urine (how they got the urine from the coyote to the bottle was a mystery to her). And if she had to, she would pinch the damn beetles off the leaves by hand.

It was slow progress, digging the trench around the garden. The ground was full of rocks, large and small, that jolted her whenever she struck them with the blade of her shovel. Before she knew it, she was down on her hands and knees with a spade, digging the stones out at close range. As she turned the soil over, earthworms writhed, and beetles fled. A tiny Armageddon. An entire world turned upside down because she wanted to plant seeds and watch them grow.

One summer when Ben was six, Anna decided that they would experiment with gardening. She'd picked up a packet of bush beans at the grocery store and planted them in the window box facing the air shaft outside Ben's room. It was messy, awkward work maneuvering around the child safety bars that protected Ben from plummeting six floors to his death. The pristine, almost fluffy potting soil flew and settled everywhere. Once planted, Ben was impatient for results.

"When's it going to come up, Mom?"

"Ben, these things take time."

"Yeah, but we put them in yesterday."

"Stop worrying. They'll come up when they're ready."

Ten days later, a sprout uncurled from the soil. Others followed. Within a month, the box was lush with promising bushes dotted with pale pink blossoms. Then something went wrong. The leaves turned ashy gray at the edges; the blossoms withered and shrank back into themselves. Ben watered the plants; Anna secretly fed them plant food, but it was no good. By the end of the summer, Ben's interest had waned, and he stopped watering the plants altogether.

When Richard returned from a business trip, Anna showed him the lifeless plants and he laughed. "Well, of course."

"What do you mean, 'of course'?"

"Well, look up. The Shapiros' air conditioner has been leaking coolant onto it all summer. It amazes me you managed to get this far."

Later, when Anna explained the problem to Ben, he just shrugged, "Stupid beans," and returned to his Legos.

The sun bore down on Anna, searing the back of her neck and soaking her t-shirt with sweat. She had been digging for an hour but had managed to open up only a few feet of the trench. Then, she remembered she had no chicken wire.

"Oh, god," she groaned as she tossed the spade to the side and rolled onto her back. She was too old for this nonsense. Her shoulders and back ached. Thank *God* that boy had rototilled the plot! What a fool she'd been to think she could do it by herself.

She closed her eyes against the sun and tried to find it, a vision of a place where she might have seen a bale of chicken wire. She recalled seeing something during their walk-through of the property. Struggling to her feet, she walked stiff-legged to the garage.

It was around at the back, she thought, a gardener's shed that extended from the building with such subtlety that you could easily miss it. Along the back wall of the shed Anna found a door with a rusty latch.

Inside, it was cool and dark. The dirt floor was packed hard from generations of use. As Anna's eyes adjusted to the dim sunlight leaking in through a dusty window, she noticed a pin-up calendar tacked to the wall. It was old, yellowing at the edges. Dated 1948, it advertised Mason's Tractor Supply. Above the sheaf of calendar pages was a studio shot of a blonde model perched on the seat of a tractor. She wore a red and white gingham two-piece bathing suit and a straw hat. Her closely held smile suggested to Anna that she might have been a local girl, maybe from the port town where the train station was.

Anna scanned the rest of the shed. A reliquary of tools hung on the walls: hand hoes, augers, rakes with warped tines, a scythe, even a harness for a horse-drawn plow. An old wooden toolbox sat on the ground and next to it in the corner, leaning against the wall as if it had been waiting for her all these years, was an ancient bale of chicken wire. She brushed aside abandoned cobwebs and started to drag the bale to the door when she noticed that the earth beneath it was different: lighter and loosely packed. When she leaned down to take a closer look, she saw the corner of a green metal box protruding from the dirt. With the help of a nearby hand hoe, she unearthed the box completely and set it on top of the toolbox.

It was an old fishing tackle box, rusty at the edges. She pried the latch open and found tiered trays inside filled with an array of flies, weights, and fishing lures whose colors had faded with time. Beneath the trays were rings of fishing line, floats, and a jackknife resting on top of a thick envelope. She wrestled the envelope out of the box and noticed it was simply labeled: *For You, with all my love.*

Anna felt as if someone was watching her; she even glanced at the open door, half expecting the addresser of the envelope to appear and snatch it from her hands. "Ridiculous," she muttered as she used the jackknife to slit the envelope open. Inside was a thick bundle of hundred-dollar bills and a letter folded around a faded photograph.

It was a picture of a pretty, young woman on a grassy beach with a lake spreading out behind her. Next to her sat a boy three or four years old holding a plastic bucket and a shovel. He was laughing as he looked at her, and she smiled back at him with a look that Anna understood completely: sheer, unabated love. The handwritten letter was dated May 22, 1999:

Babe, do you remember when you were little how much you fretted about death? I think it was around the time Grandpa's old beagle got hit by a car. You cried and all, but you were also kind of fascinated. You kept asking, "Where did his life go?" I was amazed that such a little boy could ask such big questions. Of course, this led to a lot of talk about an afterlife, and since we weren't church-goers, I didn't have much to offer you. But then you did another amazing thing: you came up with your own ideas about what happens after we die. You told stories about how if I were to die, I was to come back to you as a bird and somehow let you know it was me. Maybe you got the idea from that song I used to sing to you at bedtime. You always waved "bye-bye" to that black bird, no matter how sleepy you were.

And now, here you are, about to be a teenager. There are so many things I regret about the last twelve years. I regret that I dropped out of school. I regret that I married your father. I regret that it took so long to get away from him. I regret that I didn't protect you from him like I should have.

But I never regretted having you. I remember once you came home from school and asked me who the love of my life was. I told you to mind your own business. But you know: it's you. You are the love of my life.

There's something I've been wanting to tell you. I haven't figured out how to say it in person yet.

I know about you. I've known for years, maybe even before you knew yourself. But now you do know. I can see it. And I see that it scares you and sometimes even makes you hate yourself. Don't. Please don't. You are a good person. You deserve love—to give it and receive it—and nothing else matters. And it certainly doesn't matter fuck-all what anyone else says.

So there. See that? You made me curse.

Okay, so you know how I never trusted banks, and I certainly didn't want your father to know I had any money, so I talked to Grandpa, and we put together this little packet for you, in case you ever find yourself in need. The money comes to eight thousand dollars, and it's pretty much my entire life savings, although your grandpa chipped in a little, too.

I like it that we put all of this in his old fishing tackle box. He said you'd get a kick out of it and might remember all the times you and him went fishing at the lake before his arthritis got bad.

So that's it. That's what this is, your inheritance from him and me. Not that we're planning on going anywhere anytime soon, so don't get cocky. Years from now, we'll dig this up together and have a good laugh about what a nutty mother you have.

I love you, Babe. More than you'll ever know.

- L.

Anna sat with the box in her lap for a long time. Then she carefully placed the photograph back into the folds of the letter and returned it to its envelope next to the money. She tucked the packet back into the tackle box and latched the lid. Without thought, she carried the box into the house and placed it on the closet shelf next to Ben's boxes.

She knew what to do. After she cleaned herself up, she would drive to town to drop off the check for this month's caretaking. Maybe the boy would be there. If Richard could hire him to roto-till, she could hire him to help her put up a fence.

4

Someone had clamped an iron vise onto Richard's head. He raised a weak hand to it. Just hair, flesh, and bone. Yet every part of it—the scalp, the skull, the gray matter, each brain cell—felt as if it had been taken apart and hammered back together by an irate child. His mouth had a terrible taste—metallic, as if he had been chewing rust—and he was thirsty, so thirsty. Slowly, he opened his eyes and found himself staring at a dim room he did not recognize. He pushed himself into a sitting position and switched on a lamp.

Wherever he was, there had been a storm of thievery here. The innards of gutted sofa cushions littered the floor. Drawers of an old dresser hung slack-jawed with their contents spilling over the edges. Books had been flung about; their covers splayed like the wings of hapless birds.

Naked, Richard gathered the sheet around his waist and struggled to his feet to search for his clothes. His shoes and socks were neatly tucked under the bed, but the rest of his things were nowhere to be seen—not even his underwear. No wallet, no cellphone, no watch, no keys. Nothing. He pushed down the panic that swelled in his chest. Water. Just a glass of water. That would help. He took three shaky steps to the sink, pulled a spotty glass from the dish rack, and held it under the tap. After a long drink, he appraised his situation.

He'd been robbed—that much was clear—but how had he ended up here? Where *was* here? Had he slept through a robbery? The last thing he remembered was drinking a beer with those kids at that Irish pub on 72ⁿᵈ Street. That girl from the office—what's her name—Gina had turned out to be kind of sweet in a sad way. The others he remembered only vaguely: a trashy, neon redhead with a high-pitched laugh and a needle of a boy. And noise. There had been so much noise. And flashing lights.

He wished he knew what time it was. There was no clock in the room. No phone. Didn't people have landlines anymore? He crossed to the window and pulled back a maroon bath towel that served as a curtain. Directly across from him was another window, surrounded by grimy brick. He twisted his neck and peered up the air shaft, trying to get a glimpse of the sky. Far above was a patch of gray, nothing more. It could be seven in the morning or two in the afternoon for all he knew.

There was something he had to do today. Something at work. The taste-test trials with the new client. *Christ.*

He pawed through the dresser drawer, looking for something, anything to wear. Call Allan, make up a story, an emergency or something, a death in the fam– *no, not that, something else.* He found a green t-shirt and pulled it on. Behind him came the sound of a key in the lock. He quickly grabbed a pair of jeans and stepped into them. They were too short, baggy in the legs, tight at the waist. He sucked in his gut and managed to fasten them.

"Whatever you're looking for, it's already been stolen," a voice called. Richard turned and saw the girl, Gina, at the door. She gave him a weary smile before scanning the mess in the room and releasing a sigh. "Nice get-up," she nodded as she handed him a small paper bag.

Coffee. He pulled it out, peeled off the plastic lid, and raised the cup to his lips with shaky hands. "I didn't know how you take it," she added, watching him drink. The heat and caffeine shot right to his chest, then circled up to his brain. Clarity. He took another sip.

The girl glanced around the room again, as if at a loss, then walked to the sofa and began to re-stuff one of the cushions. Richard shuffled over to her. "Excuse me. You want to tell me what happened to my clothes?"

"Cleaners." The girl continued to work without looking up.

"'Cleaners?' What's that, code for cleaning me out? Did you give them to your friends so they could sell them?"

The girl stopped working and slowly turned to him. "No," she said, enunciating her words as if she were speaking to a dull-witted child. "I took them to the dry cleaners so they could clean off all the piss and puke."

"Whose piss and puke?"

"*Your* piss and puke. All over everything."

"Even my underwear?"

"*Especially* your underwear."

"How soon will they be ready?"

"Couple of hours."

"Jesus. I need to make a phone call."

"It was the quickest service I could get."

Richard held out his hand. "Give me your cell."

"You know, you could slip a 'please' in there," she said as she passed him her phone.

"Dear God, it's already eleven thirty. Why didn't you wake me? Allan, please. It's Richard. Yes, I'll hold. He's probably wondering where you are, too."

"I called in sick." The girl resumed her work with the cushion.

"Allan? Richard. Yes, I know. Look, I—What do you mean the webcasts aren't working? Everything you need is on my desk. Well, call Dave in Tech Services—oh, geez. All right. I'll get there as soon as I can—I know. I'm sorry, but I had a—a bit of an emergency—No, nothing serious, but—listen, just keep trying to get hold of Dave, and I'll get there pronto."

Richard turned to Gina. "Do you have any idea what a world of trouble I'm in?"

She shook her head without looking up. "Not my fault."

Richard's anger rose. "Look, I woke up this morning in this dump, stark naked and with a splitting headache. My wallet, watch, cellphone, keys—all gone."

"Were they in your jacket?"

"Yes. Why?"

"They must have been picked. Along with your jacket. When I came back for you, you were passed out on the floor –"

"What floor?"

"At the club. Don't you remember anything?"

"All I know is that right now, I'm supposed to be in a very important meeting with a new client and all *hell* is breaking loose and if I don't get over there –"

"All right! *God!*" The girl sank onto the sofa and covered her face with her hands, her shoulders shaking. She spoke through her fingers. "You know, there are some things in life that are a little more important than a stupid snack cake."

Richard bent over her. "Listen. I'm sorry. But whatever all this is," he gestured at the chaos around them, "—it has nothing to do with me. I don't belong here."

Gina raised her face to him, and there it was, the one clear memory that rose from the fog of last night, that expression through smudged eye make-up and tears of despair and forgiveness that spoke of a world he did not know.

"You're right," she said quietly. "You don't belong here. And yet, here you are."

5

Snyder's Garage sat in the center of town. "Town" struck Anna as an overstatement as it consisted of a single intersection with the gas station, a post office, a liquor store, and a bar and grill, each to a corner. There were several trucks and cars parked in front of the garage. Otherwise, there were no signs of life. Nevertheless, when Anna knocked on the office door, she heard a chair scrape the floor and footsteps shuffling. A face peered through the grimy window. "Pumps don't work. Nearest gas station is down on Route 97."

"Mr. Snyder?"

"Yeah." He opened the door a crack and squinted at the bright sunlight.

"I'm Anna Scofield. From the city?"

Nothing seemed to register as he continued to blink at her. A fine web of capillaries radiating from his nose turned a deep shade of crimson. He pulled a billed cap off his head and raked his fingers through wisps of hair the color of aged rust. The band from the cap left an indentation across his forehead. When he replaced the cap, it fit so perfectly that Anna pictured him wearing it to bed. With all his blinking and head-scratching, she was sure the caretaker had no idea who she was. "My husband and I bought the old place out on Dry Pond Road? You sent your son over this morning to cut a patch in the lawn for a garden."

He coughed and rubbed the stubble on his jaw. "Oh, yeah. Yeah." He opened the door wider and jerked his head back. Anna stepped inside.

It was dark, and the air was thick with the smell of crankcase oil. As her eyes adjusted to the dim light, she noticed half a dozen men slouched on a bench that lined the wall. They wore gray or brown work clothes darkened with grime and grease that no amount of washing would remove. She figured the men were not much older than she, but they looked awfully worn out. They said nothing in greeting, though they watched her as closely as they would a foreigner. A cooler of beer sat on the floor in front of them, next to a cairn of empty cans. "I'm sorry. I don't mean to interrupt. I just wanted to drop off a check." Snyder's eyes fluttered as if a bug had flown into them. "And I'd like to add a little extra for your son."

Snyder brushed papers, pens, and an ashtray aside to give Anna room on the desk to write the check. "He do a decent enough job?" His rheumy eyes fixed on Anna's checkbook. A chorus of grunts rippled across the men. Anna wondered if it was laughter. She could see the boy needed defending, that the men entertained themselves at his expense.

"Oh, yes." She tore out the check and handed it to Snyder. "Wonderful. In fact, I was hoping he could come out again today and help me put in the fence." She smiled and shrugged. "If he's available."

"Today, huh?" Snyder folded the check and slipped it into his shirt pocket.

"If he's not busy. I was hoping to put some peas in this weekend."

Snyder threw his head back and yelled to the air. "Hey! Knucklehead!"

"Yeah?" a voice answered from the rear of the garage.

"Whadiya doing back there? Working hard or hardly working?" This bit of wit provoked another eruption of chuckles from the men.

There was silence from the back of the garage, and then, "I'm fixing the truck."

"How much longer?"

"Don't know yet. Might have to order a part."

"How long?"

"Bout forty-five minutes."

Snyder looked at Anna. "You come back then? He'll need you to give him a lift. Truck's broke."

This was unexpected, but Anna didn't want to say anything that might make the boy look unacceptable. "That will be fine." She looked around. There was no place to sit. To wait.

"Crossroads is open for lunch. You could get a bite to eat while you wait. Food's good enough, I suppose." Snyder rubbed his paunch.

"That will be fine," Anna repeated. As she turned to leave, she looked at the clutch of men. She did it slowly, giving them time to take in her taking *them* in.

"Gentlemen," she nodded in farewell. The largest tremor yet rose and fell among them as they shifted on the bench, reached for another beer, and resettled themselves.

6

Something was wrong. There were plenty of cabs on the street, but none of them seemed to want Richard's business. As each driver slowed, peered at him through the windshield and sped away, Richard grew increasingly irate. Before he knew it, he was waving his hand and frantically shouting, "Taxi, goddammit, *taxi!*" Then he caught his reflection in a storefront window: a ragged clown in short, floppy jeans with gaping holes at the knees and an oversized green t-shirt. Perhaps the oddest component of this ensemble was the footwear of brown dress shoes and socks pleading to be taken seriously.

"Here. I'll do it." A touch on his shoulder guided him back to the curb. Gina stepped into the street, flicked her hand at a roaming cab, and drew it toward her as if she had been training it from birth.

After she settled Richard into the back seat, she pressed a wad of cash into his hand.

"This will cover your fare. I'll check on your cleaning and bring it to you at the office. Shouldn't be too long." He nodded, staring straight ahead. "Good luck, then."

The city slipped past in a blur. Richard leaned his head back and closed his eyes. His throat tightened and a shudder ran through him. He covered his face with his hand so the driver wouldn't notice if he lost control and started crying.

If only Anna was here. Not the Anna of recent years—so sharp and drawn, so quick to point out hard truths—but the Anna of long ago, the Anna who would have laughed at the absurdity of the situation and found a way to make him laugh. The Anna who would have assured him that everything was going to be all right. Perhaps an Anna he had created in his mind as he created flavors that in the end did not amount to food at all. Richard sighed, rubbed his face, and straightened up. Enough. He had to come up with a plan.

As luck would have it, the downstairs lobby of his office building was almost deserted. The doorman at the desk—Robby—recognized him after a beat and let him use the service elevator once Richard convinced him that his get-up was all part of a silly prank for a retiring coworker.

If he could only make it to his office, he could lay low and try to salvage the webcast remotely while he waited for Gina to arrive with his clothes. But when he sped past Ratna at the receptionist's desk—ignoring her sharp intake of breath—and commenced the long walk past cubicles of preoccupied workers, Richard stopped short. Heading straight toward him were Allan and the clients, deep in conversation. Richard immediately turned back, resisting an urge to crawl under a desk, and headed in the direction of the restroom. Suddenly, there was Rupert Simon, the new boss, blocking his path and bearing down on him with the determination of a bull.

Silence descended on the office. Everyone appeared to be busy at work, faces staring at monitors, fingers tapping keyboards, but it was a ruse, a masquerade of normalcy when really, covert eyes shifted to see what would happen next. "Ah, Richard. At last." Simon smiled broadly as he swung an arm around Richard's shoulders and pivoted him toward Allan and the clients.

"You're here!" Allan's eyes, wide with panic, darted from Richard to Simon. "I thought you were –"

"I can explain. Hello, Charles. Jean. Please excuse my appearance." Richard extended a hand to the clients. "It's a long story, but –"

"Well, you're here now, and that's all that matters, right?" Simon's laugh boomed across the cubicles, but his eyes, sharp as flint, bore into Richard's. He lifted his chin to the clients. "Why don't we all go up to my office? I'll have some lunch ordered, and we can go over the webcasts and see what we can do to get ourselves back on track."

Jean shook her head. "Actually, we've got to get back for a meeting." She threw a glance at her partner and cocked her head toward the door. "Charles and I will go over the results we were able to get and talk to our people. We'll get back to you in a day or two."

"We'd be happy to schedule another webcast," Allan piped. "To help, uh, clarify our findings?"

"That won't be necessary."

Sharp voices rose from the lobby and a moment later Gina, followed by a protesting Ratna, rounded the corner waving Richard's cleaning in triumph.

"They got all the piss out, but you can still smell the puke— Oh, shit. Hi, Allan."

They were quiet on the bus ride to Richard's apartment. He sat with a file box on his lap and stared at the corrugated rubber matting on the floor. Gina stood in the aisle; her eyes raised to the advertisements above the windows. From a nearby commuter grab rail hung Richard's clothes, swaying in their plastic sheath.

Richard's humiliation was complete. After the clients made their hasty departure, Simon had a few private words with Allan, security was called, and Richard was escorted to his office where he was to pack his personal belongings. There were few items to gather, just a couple of photographs and a handful of plaques and awards from the American Association of Food Flavorists. At one point, Ratna scurried in with a box she'd freed up from the supply closet, murmuring, "I'm so sorry, Richard," on her way out.

If Allan hadn't looked up, Richard might have walked past his office without stopping. But Allan did look up, lips pursed. Richard paused in his doorway. The security guards took a cautious step back. "Allan, we haven't lost this client yet," he said.

"Simon is handling it now. And as far as I'm concerned, there is no 'we.'"

"Allan, I –"

"It was a train wreck from beginning to end. And then that girl –" Allan's voice dropped to a whisper, and he leaned across his desk toward Richard. "I saw you last night. I saw you with her on the street. I don't know what kind of weird thing you're into –"

"I'm not into any kind of weird thing –"

"I don't want to discuss it! The bottom line is, I'm not going to take the fall for you. I've got two kids to put through college, a mortgage to pay off, and I'll be damned if I'm going to let your extracurricular, drugged-out, twisted, deviant activities—what the hell were you thinking, Richard?"

"Allan –"

"I don't want to discuss it!" Allan's voice rose to a squeal. The security guards stepped forward and ushered Richard out to the lobby, where Gina sat with his cleaning draped across her lap.

The super for Richard's building did not know where to look. If he took in Mr. Scofield's face, he would not be able to conceal his alarm at the dark circles and red rims that ringed the co-op board treasurer's eyes. It was a desperate, wasted look. Mr. Scofield's enormous shirt and torn pants simply confused him. If he lowered his eyes to the fancy leather shoes and dark socks, fully visible in the gap between the pants and the feet, he would burst out laughing. Then there was the girl.

Best to be discreet, to turn away and quietly honor Mr. Scofield's request for the extra key. *Who among us is without sin*, he reminded himself. But he wished the residents would behave and not put him and his crew through these awkward situations. There will be talk in the basement changing room this evening.

7

The Crossroads Bar and Grill was almost empty. The barroom was closed, and there were only two people in the diner: a wiry woman in her fifties, slicing a tomato behind the counter, and a girl, fourteen or fifteen years old, lolling on the last stool toward the back. She was pregnant, near the end of her term. An orange t-shirt strained against her protruding midriff. Below, she wore pink and green striped pajama bottoms and mismatched bedroom slippers. Strands of dirty blond hair had escaped their clip and fallen over her face. She spun slowly on the stool with her head tilted to one side, as if mesmerized by the squeak of the rotating seat. Anna noticed a yellowing bruise where the girl's cheekbone met her eye. She stopped and stared at Anna and then resumed her lazy rotations. The woman looked up from her work. "Help you?"

"Are you serving lunch yet?"

The woman shrugged and slid the tomato slices into a plastic container. "Sure. Sit anywhere you like. Menu's on the board."

Anna sat at a table along the wall and studied a dry-erase board propped up on a chair.

"Tuna on whole wheat will be fine."

"All's I got is white."

"That will be fine."

"Chips, potato salad, or coleslaw?"

"Coleslaw, I think. And a cup of coffee, please."

"Chrissy! Stop that goddamn spinning!" The woman barked without looking at the girl. The girl jerked to a halt and hung her head, awaiting her next order. The woman nodded toward the girl while keeping her eyes on Anna. "Make yourself useful."

At first, Anna thought the woman was speaking to her and wondered how she could be useful. Then the girl slid off the stool, circled behind the counter to the coffee maker, and emptied the dregs of a stale brew into the sink.

The woman worked swiftly on the sandwich, fixing her eyes on it, as if in a trance. Anna, too, fell under the spell of the woman's rhythms, then broke away and gazed around the room.

The green walls were bare, except for an illuminated sign above the counter that showed a snowboarder atop a bottle of soda charging down a mountainside. By the door to the restroom was a poster of the Twin Towers, drawn at sharp angles and standing on the insistent words, *Never Forget*.

Anna had seen this sign many times before. It was one of the earliest brandings of 9/11. You couldn't step into a deli or cleaners or liquor store in Manhattan without seeing one. Back in the days when the nation was holding its breath, it was imperative to remember the dead, to speak their names and read their stories in The New York Times, to have them live among us just a little longer.

Richard had been traveling that day and was stranded in Dallas, waiting for air travel to resume. Anna stayed with her students as their parents arrived in dribs and drabs. Many of them had hiked the seven miles from Wall Street and wore the dazed and ragged expressions of neo-refugees.

By the time Anna left the school there was only one student remaining. She was sitting in the Head's office, strangely frozen in the powder blue armchair, staring into space, her fingertips pressed lightly against her lips as if to contain the dreadful realization.

As she walked through Central Park toward Ben's high school

on the Upper West Side, Anna paused to look south across the reservoir. The silver skyline glistened against a brilliant blue sky. Beyond the midtown buildings hung a heavy plume of dirty yellow smoke. The air held an acrid odor. It was the smell of *that*. All of it: smoldering concrete and steel, shattered glass, diesel fuel, electrical wires and duct work, insulation, office furniture, fluorescent lights, computers, papers, briefcases, purses.

People.

A soft wind urged the smoke upward.

Ben was hanging out on the front steps of his school with a group of his friends. When he saw Anna, he broke away and loped over to her. "Did you hear that a couple of guys tried to wire the GW Bridge?" He pranced around her like a boxer.

"What? Where'd you hear that?"

"Someone said. And a truck bomb exploded at the Pentagon."

"I heard it was another plane."

"Whatever. No school tomorrow."

"Let's go home. I want to get off the streets."

"Oh, c'mon, Mom. What, do you think people will riot? Do you think the enemy is going to swim across the Hudson holding knives in their teeth? It's not like we live in a war zone." Anna kept her mouth shut and looked up as another fighter jet roared above Manhattan.

Amazingly, they could still order Chinese takeout. That evening they sat on the sofa and ate directly out of the boxes while they watched the local news anchors flounder behind their desks.

"Geez, look at them," Ben said.

"They don't know what to call it yet. They don't have a name for it."

"They look scared shitless."

Later, after Ben holed himself up in his room to IM with

his friends, Anna went for a short walk in Riverside Park. At the Firemen's Memorial people were gathered with lighted candles to lay flowers and written messages at the foot of the fountain basin. They stood in silence, their heads bent, each alone in thought but needing the company of others. Anna sat on a stone bench next to a young woman who reached over and took her hand. She was not sure if the girl was asking for or offering comfort. Maybe both. And so, she held this stranger's hand and said nothing in this communion of sorrow beyond words.

"God Bless America! What the hell do you think you're doing?" Anna turned her head in time to see the woman behind the counter flick a sharp backhand at the girl's head. The girl yelped and ducked out of range. Somehow, she had bungled the coffee. Brown water, thick with grounds, spilled onto the back counter and floor. "Go get the mop." The girl was slow to move in such tight quarters. The woman threw a wet, gritty dishrag at her. "Go on, goddammit!

"Stop it!" the girl whined.

The woman shot a furtive glance at Anna and then leaned into the girl. In a fierce whisper, she hissed, "You shut up and get that mop right now or I don't know what."

The girl turned and ambled toward the back. As she passed by, Anna heard her mutter, "*You* shut up."

There was nowhere safe to look. No newspaper or book to bury her face in as she would on the subway where there was safety in numbers. At the school, she would have been required to report such an incident to her director, perhaps even to call Child Protective Services. But she was no longer a teacher. Nothing was required of her, so she was rudderless. She hunched over her paper placemat and read the little ads for trash removal, tree-cutting, the pumping of septic tanks.

After a few minutes, there was the woman standing next to the table with a paper plate. She set it down in front of Anna: a tuna sandwich, a mound of coleslaw weeping its juice, and a fan of pickle chips. "Coffee'll be a bit."

Anna glanced at the girl, who was now half-heartedly pushing a mop back and forth behind the counter. "Oh, that's fine. I prefer to have it after anyway." She felt stiff. Too proper. The woman heaved an exhausted sigh and dropped onto a stool at the counter. Anna picked up her sandwich and took a small bite.

"You're not from around here, are you?"

Anna swallowed her food. "No. We live in the city. We just bought a place out on Dry Pond Road. The Reynolds' house?"

"Oh, yeah. Well, Reynolds was just a blip. The real owner was Hans Mueller. He built the place. Crazy old man. Wasn't a creature that could walk across his property without getting shot and dumped into the stewpot or stuffed and mounted on the wall."

"Yes. There's quite a collection of taxidermy."

"Our folks always said, 'If you go over to the Muellers', don't eat the stew.' You never knew what was in it: squirrel, raccoon, possum. Could'a been skunk for all we knew."

The woman allowed a silence to grow while she watched Anna eat. She stretched her arm out along the counter and drummed her fingers on it, lost in thought.

"This is delicious," Anna said between bites. It wasn't, but she figured she would eat it up and get out of there. She would wait for the boy in her car.

"So, how do you like it?"

Anna swallowed. "I'm sorry. I guess my mouth was full. I like it. I said it was good."

"No. This place. Our little town."

"Oh. It's—I don't know much about it yet. It's pretty. So quiet and peaceful. Nice not to have to lock your doors at night."

"What makes you think you don't have to lock your doors at night?"

"Well, I mean, in the city, we lock everything up. People even chain their potted plants to their stoops."

"I wouldn't go to bed without my doors locked. Things happen." The woman leaned in toward Anna and cocked her head toward the girl. "Lotta inbreeding around here."

Anna watched the girl resume her spinning on the counter stool. When it squeaked, she stopped and reversed direction and made it squeak again. "She isn't yours?"

"Hell, no. She's my niece. By marriage," she emphasized. "She lives with her dad, who can't seem to figure out what to do with her. So, he dumps her off with me from time to time, like she's supposed to be a help around here."

Anna nodded and took another bite. There was so much she could ask about, so much that was clear to the eye. Like that bruise. And the baby the girl would bear in about a month, if Anna were any judge. But she didn't want to get drawn in.

"Your crime rate must be low."

"Oh, sure, it's low. Nothing like what you got in the city, I suppose. Usually 'bout the worst thing that happens here is a bunch of teenagers go joyriding at night and whack a few mailboxes with baseball bats."

"So, that's not so bad."

"'Course, every once in a while, something crazy happens."

"Really."

The girl was twisting back and forth quickly now, as the stool emitted a series of rapid squeals. The woman shot her a dirty look, then returned her attention to Anna. "We had a murder a few years back."

"Oh—dear."

"Crazy guy about thirty-eight years old. Lived with his father, who was a son of a bitch in his own right. Kept to themselves, especially after the mother ran off. You could tell there was something off about the son. Used to wander through people's yards and mess with their pets or break into their houses when they wasn't home and drink the beer out of their refrigerators." A particularly loud screech echoed through the diner. "*Enough!*" the woman hollered at the girl. The child stopped immediately and slumped over the counter.

"So, what happened?" Anna couldn't help herself.

"Well, it was night. Middle of the summer. Hot as Hades. A woman and her son were sleeping on their sunporch, trying to keep cool, I suppose. This guy breaks in and tries to rape the woman. The boy—he was about twelve—runs and gets a knife out of the kitchen. Some kind of struggle takes place—no one knows for sure exactly what happened—but somehow the guy gets hold of the knife and cuts up the boy real bad. The boy manages to escape and runs over to a neighbor's place about a half mile away. By the time the constable gets out to the house, the mother is dead, and there's no sign of the guy. They found him a few hours later, wandering the woods, covered with blood."

"Dear God."

"So, I'd lock my doors if I was you."

"Where is he now?"

"Oh, he's doing life. He confessed everything. He'll never get out."

"No. I mean the boy."

The woman shrugged. "He stayed with his dad for a while, who's a useless drunk. Then his grandfather took him in but –" She stopped suddenly and covered her mouth with her hand.

"What?"

The woman released a breath of laughter. "Well, I'll be damned. I forgot who I was talking to."

"Me?"

"Yeah, you. Your place.

"I—what do you mean, 'my place?'"

"Hans Mueller. He was the grandfather. It was his daughter who was killed. The kid stayed with him for a couple of years. In that house. Then Mueller got sick. He was pretty old by then, and the kid started getting into trouble at school—fights and such—so they sent him off to New Jersey, I think. Stayed with friends of friends or some distant relations. I'm not sure. Finished out high school down there, I guess. He's back now."

With a shiver, Anna remembered the tackle box and letter she'd found in the shed. She considered telling the woman about it. But no. She was not willing to give up the secret yet, not to anyone, certainly not to this fuming gossip. "He's back here?"

"Yeah. Back with his father, for all the good it does him."

"Because he's –?"

"Man's a waste of oxygen. Has to jumpstart hisself with a six-pack every morning just to get out of bed."

"You know a lot about him."

"I oughta. I went out with him for about five seconds after him and his wife split up. He still bad-mouths her, even though she's dead. Right in front of the kid. Personally, I liked her. She was real sweet. Want me to wrap the rest of that up for you?"

"No, no. That's okay. I'll skip the coffee and just take the check."

"By the way…" The woman rang up the bill. "…got a back-up generator?"

"A what?"

"We get a lot of outages up here, what with blizzards and thunderstorms. Wind kicks up pretty bad. Good idea to have a generator for backup."

"No, I don't think we have plans for that."

"Be a good idea. My brother-in-law sells them. He could set you up."

Anna wondered if this was the same brother-in-law who couldn't handle his pregnant daughter. Who gave her that shiner. "Well, I'd have to talk to my husband."

"Be a good idea. You set up with flashlights and batteries? Crank radio?"

Anna shook her head. "Not really."

"Keep your candles in the freezer. Makes them burn longer. That's a trick they taught us in the military."

"Right now, I'm putting in a vegetable garden for the summer."

The woman threw her head back and moaned. "Oh, well, now you're talkin' frustration. Between the woodchucks and the deer, it'll be a wonder if you get out of it what you put into it."

"Yes, I know. But I've been researching ..." Anna was embarrassed to reveal her lack of common wisdom, that she was from the city and had to read articles to understand the simplest concepts. "I'm building a fence. A high one. I've got the boy across the street helping me."

"Really?" The woman gave Anna a sharp look.

"Well, it's a simple enough job. He already turned over the sod. He seems like a good worker."

The woman kept looking at Anna, with suspicion, it seemed. Would she be gossiping about her to the next customer who strolled in, just to entertain herself? Anna no longer cared. She could give as good as she got. "By the way," Anna nodded toward the girl. "How did she get that bruise?"

The woman held her look. Didn't even blink. "She's a clumsy girl," she said in even tones. "You've seen as much."

8

Gina couldn't wait to get into the apartment. She had to pee something fierce but tried not to show it. She was tired, bone tired after a brutal night and day filled with dread and resignation that still pulsed through her like a low-grade fever. Every decision she had made, every attempt to set things right had crashed and burned. Now the super, smiling and embarrassed, fumbled with the keys until he finally opened the door and let them in.

The apartment was quiet and neat, uncluttered in a cleaning-service kind of way. Gina felt as if she'd stepped into a residential museum. The colors of the walls and furnishings were muted earth tones that probably had names like 'Mountain Laurel,' 'Stream Silt,' and 'Terra Firma.' The polished end tables flanking the sofa displayed upscale knickknacks: a green marble egg perched on a silver pedestal, crystal coasters, and a tarnished copper urn bought at some antique shop in Connecticut, no doubt. It was unnerving, the way each little item had its place. *Who lives like this?* She turned to Richard. "Bathroom?" He led her down the hall without a word and pointed to a door on the right before continuing to the bedroom and shutting himself inside.

It was an enormous bathroom by Gina's standards. As she sat on the toilet and enjoyed an unbelievably long piss, she took in the vanity with two sinks set in a marble countertop. It was easy to guess which was *His* and which was *Hers*. *His* was devoid of any kind of clutter, save a pewter dish holding a perfect, unused bar of goat's milk soap. *Hers* was a bit of a mess, bordered with an array of lotions, face creams, tweezers, and a sour-smelling washcloth sitting in a heap, just the kind of thing that must drive *Him* nuts.

After Gina flushed, she ran the water in *Her* sink to wash her hands and mask the scrape of the mirrored door of the medicine cabinet as she slid it open. Again, *His* and *Her* sides. There were his toiletries. No big surprises: shaving cream and a razor, aftershave, nail clippers, blood pressure medicine. *Her* side was a continuation of the same stuff that was on the countertop, except—what was this? Zoloft? Gina reached for the bottle, and as soon as she touched it, she knew it was empty.

If Lexi were here, she'd be so disappointed. Disappointed enough to steal something, anything that would take the sting out of the disappointment. Gina had seen her do it. In fact, Lexi loved to make Gina watch her steal: in drugstores, at the market, even from street vendors in their own neighborhood. Lexi made an art of thievery, choosing the perfect thing, sometimes based on aesthetics, sometimes based on risk. The deeper the disappointment, the riskier the filch. It wasn't out of need. She couldn't plead poverty. Not with her daddy up in Westchester footing the rent for the apartment and sending her a monthly allowance and whatever else it took to keep her out of his hair. Lexi always said she stole to keep her "skills honed," but Gina knew that she did it for the same reason she drank, tried any drug that came within reach, took up with creeps like Nat, and hopped from one thing to another like a flea on speed. She was looking for a place to rest. She was looking for the one thing that would slow her down, allow her to breathe and fill that gaping hole of loneliness inside her.

Gina had been stupid enough to think she could fill that hole, and for a while, hadn't she? It was the least she could do after Lexi had brought her in from the streets, offered her a roof and a bed. In that little apartment, they cooked cheap meals of fried rice and vegetables and laughed and kept each other warm at night. After a while, Lexi let down her guard enough to tell Gina about her awful family: the father and the stepmother and all the little step-brats who hoped she'd stay put on the Lower East Side, even on holidays. Gina knew something about that. So, she listened as an act of love. These stories were small gems that Gina held close. Little nuggets of light and dark that told the truth about life. She held Lexi, naked against her own nakedness, and they cried and laughed to see who could tell the saddest story.

Gina replaced the medicine bottle, slid the door shut, and turned off the tap. She stared at her reflection. What a mess. Her electric hair had lost its charge and hung limp, and in this light the pink streaks took on a sallow, orange cast. The eyeliner on one lower lid was smeared and matched the dark circles under her eyes. She was getting older. *Too old for this shit.* Yet here she was: homeless again, jobless again, and no plan in sight.

Slowly, she removed her hardware: the studs lining her ears, the rings in her nose, lips, and brow. Without them, she looked younger, a little more like her old self—a Catholic schoolgirl from New Jersey—except for that furrow between her brows that first appeared when her mother got sick and had only deepened over the last couple of years. It would be there for the rest of her life.

She opened the door to the bathroom and stuck her head outside. "Hey," she called. "Mind if I take a bath?" No answer, although she could hear the low tones of Richard talking on the phone. She shut the door to the bathroom, turned the lock, and started to fill the tub. There was a jar of bath salts on *Her* side of the sink. Gina pulled off the large cork stopper and poured a good amount into the tub. As steam rose from the water, a memory of her mother flashed before her, sitting in the tub at home, her body bent and waiting while Gina swirled Epsom salt into the water.

She had become silent, her mother, during the last weeks of her life. No more fear, no more confessions uttered during the darkest hours of the night while Gina held her hand and stroked the few wisps of hair left on her scalp. Finally, she resigned herself to the claim that illness made on her body. And with her resignation came a sense of peace, as if the worries and fears that she'd harbored all her life had drifted out to sea. As Gina sponged her mother's back, the skin—loose from weight loss—shifted like floating islands. Her mother would turn to her and smile the sweetest smile, so sweet that it made the horror go away for a moment.

When the water reached a good depth, Gina turned off the faucet, shed her clothes, and stepped into the tub. The water was hot, as hot as she could bear. She leaned back and allowed it to close over her. The scent of the bath salts rose with the steam and reminded her of oranges and tea. She closed her eyes, and slowly the knots in her body began to uncoil.

He had been fine leaving Allan's office. Fine walking past Ratna in reception, fine in the elevator and in the lobby, fine walking to the bus stop, fine letting the girl pay his fare, fine climbing off the bus and walking the two blocks to his building, fine explaining to Manny that he'd lost his keys, fine riding up to the sixth floor and watching Manny let him and the girl in, fine showing the girl the way to the bathroom, and fine stepping into his bedroom. All of that had been fine.

But once the door shut, the perfect order of his desk stared back at him in bleak reproach and a wave of panic broke over him. His knees buckled. He groped for his bed, crawled onto it, and curled into the tightest ball his girth would allow. He wished he could weep. Crying would have been a relief, but his body would not allow it. It seized up, then released, seized and released. From a distance, it seemed, he heard a strange, moaning sound that he stifled when he held a pillow against his mouth.

When it was finally over and his breathing returned to normal, he climbed out of bed and began to peel off the ridiculous clothes he was wearing. The t-shirt had some kind of writing on the back that he hadn't noticed before. He laid it out on the bedspread and read: **Don't be a dick.**

Perfect, thought Richard. No wonder they'd called security.

He put on his robe and sat down at his desk.

The computer, phone, and pile of this month's bills all charged him with one simple mission: *minimize the damage.* He pulled some files from the drawer and began his calls to the credit card companies. At one point, the girl called out to him. He didn't hear what she said, and he didn't care. Since she didn't call again, he let it drop. *Later,* he told himself. He would deal with her later. Thank her and send her on her way. Right now, there were more pressing matters to deal with.

The water in the tub had cooled and was no longer a comfort. Gina stood and reached for a towel. She did not want to put on her clothes. They lay in a heap on the floor, damp with the sweat, grim, and tension of last night. Instead, she reached for a white robe that hung from a hook. It belonged to *Her,* she imagined. A little tight for Gina but not so small that she couldn't overlap it and secure it with the sash. *Her* wouldn't mind, she imagined.

The door to the bedroom was still closed, so Gina padded through the living room to the kitchen and opened the door to the refrigerator. So clean and politically correct: red pepper hummus and goat cheese from Zabar's, brown eggs from "hormone-and-antibiotic-free-uncaged chickens," organic skim milk, and a bunch of kale—locally grown, no doubt. Although hunger churned in her gut, there was absolutely nothing here that she wanted to eat. Sleep was what she needed. She closed the fridge with a sigh and wandered down the hall to what looked like a den.

There was a daybed along two windows that overlooked an air shaft. Above a small desk on the opposite wall hung a collection of family photographs. Most of them showed a boy, from birth to now, she supposed. And there was *Her, She, The Owner of the Bathrobe. The Lady of the House.* Gina leaned in to take a closer look.

Her was so...ordinary. Medium height and build, brown hair that she wore long in the younger pictures but as the boy grew older, *Her* had settled on a bob that reached just to her shoulders. Gina's own mother had done the same, she supposed, although she'd never seen photos of her as a girl. Why do women do that? she wondered. Give up on long hair and cut it short for the middle-ages and beyond? While *Her* was not a stunner, she came to life whenever the boy appeared in a picture with her. It was as if he supplied her with her life force. And he was a doll, with big brown eyes and blond curls that gradually turned brown as he grew older. There was an awkward phase around thirteen, but it looked as if he had managed to pull through by the time he graduated from high school. During those years, there was also a change in the dynamic between the boy and *Her.* Instead of the free-flowing love that passed between them in their younger days, now he leaned slightly away from *Her,* his smile tight, his hands jammed into his jeans' pockets. And where was Richard all these years? Always behind the camera? Gina scanned the wall and found one shot of the three of them, the boy—now tall and handsome—in a cap and gown holding his high school diploma, *Her* at his side, smiling and proud, and Richard at his other side, stiff and slightly apart from them, as if he'd been rented for the occasion.

Well, at least they've got their family dysfunction on film. Gina only had an archive of memories that filled her with doubts and sadness. Several weeks after her mother died, Gina cooked up a week's worth of casseroles for the freezer and announced to her father one evening over dinner at the kitchen table—their 'Last Supper' she'd come to call it—that she was a lesbian.

His response was no surprise. He tightened his grip on his can of Bud and stared at his Sloppy Joe and peas. Finally, he said, "I figured as much. You'll be leaving then."

"I've got my bags packed."

"Did your mother know?"

"I never said a word."

"Thank God for that, at least."

"I'll send you my address once I get one."

"Don't see why. I'll just throw it in the trash."

"That's it, then, Dad? Just shut the door and bolt it? No Christmas cards? No get-togethers at Thanksgiving?"

The muscles in his jaws clenched a moment, and Gina was sure he was about to pop but this one time he managed to control himself and simply answered, "That's it."

She got up from the table while he remained. When she left the kitchen, he was lifting the hamburger bun to his mouth, spilling ground beef and catsup onto his hands. He hadn't moved his eyes from his plate, not once.

She moved out that night.

Life on the streets hadn't been so bad. But then, she hadn't been out there that long, not long enough to take on that layer of grime and hollow-eyed fatigue. Not long enough to deal with winter and shelters and cops and hunger and all the other hazards that plagued lifers. Lexi hadn't even guessed Gina was homeless when they'd first met. Hell, Gina hadn't thought of herself that way, just...between residences. Which is probably what saved her, her refusal to see herself on a downward slide. When Lexi plopped down next to her on that park bench on a hot afternoon in August hoping to score some weed, they met as equals. More or less.

Lexi had given her a roof, an address, a place to cook and clean, a place to leave in the morning and to come home to at night. A nest. And Gina had given Lexi companionship, an ear, a shoulder, an open heart. What a fool she had been to think it was love.

The weight of Gina's exhaustion grew heavy. She lay down on the daybed and pulled a throw over her. Had this been the boy's room once? Where did he live now? There was no trace of him here, save the photos and perhaps that framed painting on the wall with its childlike splashes of all the colors in the world. Gina closed her eyes and tried to quiet her mind, the only part of her that fought sleep.

She would not go back to her apartment. Last night, after she'd put Richard to bed, she went out again to look for Lexi. For hours she searched the streets: their favorite bars, the dark corner in the park where she knew Lexi had started dealing. She finally found her in the abandoned building where Nat squatted. The two of them lay flat out on his crappy mattress, half-naked, sleeping off their high. On the floor next to Lexi's limp arm was the small, zippered pouch in which Gina kept her savings. She had hidden it in the apartment behind some books on a shelf, the last place she'd imagined Lexi would look. But Lexi was a determined little user. Seven hundred dollars. Gina had gradually stashed it away over the last several months. Emergency money. A lifeline. And now two hundred of them were gone, exchanged for the chemicals that coursed through Lexi's veins, eating their way through her last few good brain cells. Gina watched Lexi's chest rise and fall in a slow, even rhythm. Nat stirred, dropped open his jaw and resumed snoring. At least they were alive. This time.

Next to her money pouch, Gina found a syringe, a tarry spoon, lighter, rubber tie-off, and two small plastic bags: one empty and one full. For later. She emptied the bag of white powder onto the floor and rubbed it into the planking with her foot. Then she picked up the works and threw them out the broken window. The money went into her pocket. The last thing she did before she left was to pull a loose strand of hair out of Lexi's mouth.

It was a bad time now. Gina felt as if she was standing at the edge of her life. There had been bad times before, and she had survived them. She would survive these bad times. She cast her mind ahead ten years, twenty, thirty years. Who would she be at thirty-two, forty-two, an impossibly far away fifty-two? It *was* a bad time now, but it would not always be bad—not *this* bad.

Near the end of her life, when she could still speak but was half-mad with pain and medications, Gina's mother confessed her great guilt, the secret of another life, a life before Gina, even before Gina's father. She spoke in half-sentences and garbled words, but Gina was able to piece together the gist of it: an earlier marriage to a violent man, a troubled son who took on his father's brutish ways, her mother's escape from rural upstate New York to the suburbs of New Jersey, of all places and eventually to a new life with Gina's father. She had escaped bad times and remade her life, her mother. While it hadn't been ideal—hobbled by her gift for attracting brooding, taciturn men with mean streaks—she had survived. And she had given birth to Gina, a girl whom she had loved fiercely. Gina believed in this and held it close as she finally drifted off to sleep.

9

The brilliance of the day had faded by the time Anna stepped out of the diner. The sky held low-hanging clouds the color of lead, and she was struck by a prickly stillness in the air as she walked to her car.

Across the road, the bay to Snyder's garage was open. Parked inside was the red pickup truck that she'd seen in her driveway that morning. Its hood was open, and the lower half of the boy's body was visible as he leaned over the engine, tinkering. Snyder and his cronies crowded around and watched. Every so often a chorus of guffaws erupted from the group, and Anna imagined they were poking fun at the boy. Suddenly, he did a little hop, and his feet hung suspended over the ground as he balanced his body on the fender, his hips the fulcrum and his upper body hidden by the open hood. From where Anna stood, it looked as if the truck was devouring him. She turned away and continued toward her car.

What was Richard doing? she wondered. Right now. Friday afternoon. Whenever Anna thought of Richard in his office, she always imagined him slowly turning his chair to take in his view of the Manhattan skyline.

But what the hell did he do all day? How did he keep going? Didn't he ever find his mind drifting? Hadn't he ever found himself subject to little rages or unexpected tears in the middle of some meeting? If Richard had mourned during this past year, he'd done a good job of hiding it. For a while, she thought he was just trying to be strong for her sake, to protect her from his grief. But any attempts she made to draw him out were met with irritated dismissals, as if she had said something in bad taste.

They fought about this. Just the other night, out of sheer frustration she held it up to him, like a prized pelt. Dropped it at his feet. It was a terrible offering. He tried to ignore it, but she kept nudging it in front of him. Finally, in an exasperated tone, he said, "Yes, Anna, I feel grief. I feel pain. I, too, mourn Ben's death."

"How would I know? You never talk about it. You're so damn chipper all the time."

"What do you want me to do? Put on a show for you? Share *everything* with you? Am I not allowed any privacy?"

"I'm not talking about taking out a full-page ad in The Times, Richard. I'm your wife, not some random stranger."

Richard turned and walked toward the bedroom, muttering under his breath.

She followed him. "What? What did you say?"

"Nothing."

She pulled his arm. "Come on. Say it."

He turned to face her. "I said it would be easier if you were some random stranger."

"Why? Why would that be easier?"

"Because I could walk away. I could walk away from a random stranger and never have to talk about it again. Because a random stranger wouldn't have known Ben and loved him so much more than I did."

"You loved Ben."

"Not like you. No one could love him as much as you." He held up a forgiving hand. "I understand. A mother and her son. That's a special thing, a special bond."

"You were always traveling. Ben and I spent a lot of time alone together."

"I understand. I'm just saying that when I did come home, there never seemed to be very much room for me."

"When you came home, you always tried to control everything. 'Why is he dressed like that? Does he have to slouch so much? I don't like his tone of voice.' If he left his backpack or jacket in the living room, you always had to make a comment. You were like a dog, pissing on everything, marking territory."

"You coddled him."

"You belittled him."

Richard took a sharp breath and let it out slowly. "You always took his side. You never, *never* backed me up. The two of you ganged up on me. It was as if you formed this secret club that I could never join."

"You're blaming me for being close to Ben. What did you expect? I can't help it if you didn't put in the time, Richard. What was I supposed to do? *Not* fill the void? Hit pause until you returned? He needed to grow up with some sense of family, even if it was just me."

They were standing in the hallway between the bathroom and the bedroom. There was no light save for a bit of spill from the lamp on the nightstand. Even so, Anna could see Richard's face redden and his eyes waver as he stared at her. Without a word, he went into their room to get ready for bed, shutting the door behind him. That night, like so many other nights lately, she slept in Ben's old room.

As Anna opened the door of her car, she heard raised voices from the garage. They were arguing, the boy and Snyder. Suddenly, the men burst out of the bay like a raffle of turkeys and scattered to their cars and pickups. As they drove off in all directions, Anna heard the crash of metal on metal, more cursing, and then the boy emerged from the garage, walking fast toward her, his fists jammed into the pockets of his hoodie and a grim expression on his face. Snyder appeared at the door with a wrench in one hand and a can of beer in the other.

"Well, you fucked that up!" he bellowed. "Just like you fuck up everything else, you son of a bitch bastard!" He staggered a bit and hurled the can at the boy. It flipped end over end and smashed onto the road in an explosion of foam and brew.

The boy kept his eyes locked on Anna. When he got to the car, he yanked the passenger door open and ducked inside. Anna slid in on her side. The boy sank into his seat as if he wanted to disappear into his clothes. She looked back and saw Snyder making an unsteady but murderous advance toward the car, wrench in hand. The boy did not need to look back.

"Go," he growled.

Anna buckled up, slipped the key into the ignition and turned it, shifted to drive, then hesitated. In the side-view mirror, she saw Snyder closing in.

The boy twisted his head toward her. "Go. *Please!*"

"Seatbelt."

He stared at her for a moment, then reached for the seatbelt. As soon as she heard it click, Anna floored it. The car leapt forward with a shriek. In the rear-view mirror, a diminishing Snyder cursed and shook his wrench at them. She laughed at the sight. As they rounded the bend, the thrill of escape fueled the surge forward. Anna glanced at the boy and saw a small grin light his face as he stared wide-eyed at the road ahead. A rush of conspiratorial glee pulsed through her. Suddenly, she was a girl again, holding hands with a boy and running, running, running from the ugliness of stupid adults and the fucked-up world they'd made.

10

After they transferred trains at Secaucus Junction, Richard tried to reach Anna again on Gina's cellphone and again got her voicemail. He left yet another message, this one with a trace of impatience in his voice. She must be in the garden or the village or hiking in the woods or any number of possibilities. He shifted in his seat, trying to find the least uncomfortable position and leaned his head against the window.

He had done everything he knew to do back at the apartment: reported his stolen credit cards, left a message for his lawyer to see if he could get his job back or at least negotiate a better severance package. The son of a bitch had left his office early to head up to the Berkshires for the weekend. Maybe Richard should have gone to law school back when he was casting his lines into the future. Those guys always have work. But Richard? Where was he going to find another job at his age? He was barely managing to keep up with the twenty-and thirty-somethings whose fluency with the latest technology left him feeling sluggish and old.

He glanced at Gina in the seat opposite his, her back against the direction of the train. She was turned toward the window, eyes shuttered, caught in a nether region of fatigue, her head nodding, then snapping back to wakefulness only to nod off again. What will Anna say when she meets her? He had enough explaining to do. His world had been knocked from its axis and was spinning so wildly off-orbit that he no longer recognized it. Anna would pull him back in. She was his gravity. But for now, it was Gina who kept him tethered to earth, fragile though that bond was.

Back in the apartment when he finally emerged from the bedroom, he'd found the girl napping in the den, wearing Anna's robe. He shook her awake, a little more roughly than he'd intended.

"What?" The girl sat up on the bed, yawning, and ran her fingers through her hair. She looked different to him somehow, younger.

"What do you think you're doing?"

"I'm resting."

"You just come into someone's house and take their clothes and make yourself at home?"

"What the hell? You came into *my* place and took *my* clothes and made *yourself* at home."

"That was different."

"Why? Because I also brought you coffee and picked up your cleaning after you made a royal mess of yourself?"

"Okay. *Okay.*"

"You gotta stop this shit." She stared at him, studying him.

He gathered himself for an apology. "If I have offended you, then it is regrettable."

"Are you kidding? You sound like you're reading from the HR manual. You *have* offended me. There's no *if* about it."

"Well, then. If –"

"Stop saying 'if.' This is not theory. This is practice."

"I don't –"

"It's like saying, 'mistakes were made.' No. *I* made a mistake. *You* made a mistake. *We* made a mistake. Stop dodging."

He had heard these words before. Or words very much like them. Anna had said the same thing several times over the years. Richard dropped his head. "I'm sorry."

"I forgive you."

"I'm afraid I need another favor." He took a deep breath. "See, I've got to get up to my wife," he began. "We have a country house a couple of hours away. She's there, and she's expecting me. Obviously, we've got a lot to talk about." He was waiting for the girl to interrupt him, but she just listened. Nobody ever listened to him anymore. "I thought I might rent a car but with my wallet gone, I don't have a license or credit cards. But you could rent a car –"

"Nope."

Richard snapped his mouth shut and turned to her. "What do you mean, 'nope'?"

"What do you mean what do I mean?"

"I mean you can't, or you won't?"

"Can't. I don't drive."

Richard shook his head. "How can you not drive?"

Gina sighed. "You know, you really ought to get out more. A lot of people—people *I* know—don't drive. We don't need it. We get around just fine.

"Okay...so, what?"

"I like trains."

"The thing is, I don't have any means, any money –"

"I have money. I happen to be carrying an unusually large amount of money. For me, anyway. A few hundred. And I've got about eight credit cards in my wallet."

"Eight?"

"The banks keep mailing me credit card offers. I must get about five a week. Zero percent interest for six months. It's crazy how badly they want me to go into debt."

"But why so many? Aren't you afraid of—you know..."

"...of getting in over my head? I don't *use* the damn things. I just have them. In case I get into a jam or if a friend's wallet is pinched and he needs to get to his wife at his country house.

He laughed. "So, you'll lend me a little?"

"I'll do better than that. I'll go with you."

"No –"

"Don't even try to argue. How are you going to use my credit cards without me?" Her smile faded and to his surprise, he saw the need in her. "I've got no place else to go. My job's gone too, you know. And my home. My whole life is right there in that bag." She gestured to the black bicycle messenger bag on the floor and shook her head as if to shake off her sadness. "Right now, what I need is a project. And that project is you."

Gina had fallen fully asleep by now; her head leaned back against the window and vibrated slightly from the movement of the train. Odd to see her in Anna's clothes. Gina hadn't wanted to wear her own. 'Too skanky,' she said. So, they dug through Anna's closet and found a box labeled "Fat Clothes." After a few dry comments about women and body image, Gina settled on a pair of black jeans and a navy cable knit turtleneck. She looked sweet, except for her biker boots and leather jacket she insisted on wearing.

The train passed through a tunnel and emptied into a world of freeways, parking lots, and abandoned brick warehouses speckled with broken windows. Oh, these sad American towns. Richard knew that trains always saw the backside of any place, but if you were to judge from this vantage point, you would swear the country was falling apart, descending into a state of decay with its litter-strewn landscapes of empty playgrounds and graffitied fences. Soon they rattled past an expanse of spindly woods with crumbling stone walls that swerved up and down the countryside, marking ancient and irrelevant boundaries. Richard shifted his weight and tried to ease a cramp in his leg.

He recalled the trains in old black and white movies with their dining cars boasting crisp, white tablecloths and real silverware and porcelain dishes. He remembered the trains of his childhood: the mournful wail of the whistle and the rumble of the wheels as they sped by, just two blocks from his house. The pennies he put on the tracks and picked up later after a passing train flattened them into copper smears.

For his seventh birthday, his mother took him and a few of his friends on the train to Endicott. They went to Fowler's Department store and rode the escalator—his first time on one—until the floor manager made a nasty remark, suggesting they leave. The train ride home seemed so much longer, the boys quiet, his mother looking out the window with the back of her hand pressed against her lips.

Then there was the ride from the city to the Hamptons. It was the beginning of the summer of 1980, and the train was packed with affluent young suits, singles heading out for a weekend at their summer timeshares. Girls with torsos like triangles: padded shoulders and cinched waists. They wore sneakers and socks with their skirts. The party had already started on the train, but he sat quietly with his face turned to the window.

So many false starts. So many jobs that just hadn't panned out, even after he'd earned his MBA. He was tapped out. Done. So, when Toby, his old college roommate, asked for help with the book-keeping and management of his new restaurant in Southampton, Richard thought, *why the hell not?*

Funny. He hadn't thought much of Anna at first. She was just a girl, one of a handful who worked on the waitstaff. A green girl, fresh out of college with no aspirations, home for the summer until she figured out what to do with her life. She was quiet. At a chance meeting in the kitchen, she might look up from her work and return a hello or might just keep her eyes fixed on her pile of napkin roll-ups and say nothing. Not that Richard was any standout.

Several years older than Anna, a little less naïve, perhaps but still flying by the seat of his pants.

Then there was that night. They had all gone to a bar after work—the whole crew—to blow off steam. Anna was playing pool in the back room. Still dressed in her black and whites; her vest trimmed her figure with a smart snap. Richard sat at a table in the corner and watched her as he half-listened to the conversations around him.

She played the game like a pro, with focus and purpose. There was nothing flirty about her. She didn't drink or dance between shots or giggle at her mistakes. She wasn't doing it to exhibit herself. She just played like, well, like there was money at stake. At one point, Toby came up behind her, beer in hand, pressed into her and whispered some joke into her ear. She just shook him off and kept her eyes on the game. "Guess she doesn't like me anymore," he said loud enough for her to hear. He slouched into a chair at Richard's table. "Just as well." He took a long pull from his beer and leaned in. "Wanna know why I like younger women?" He chuckled and swung his head toward Anna. "Their stories are shorter."

"Yeah?" Richard replied, also loud enough for Anna to hear. "Sort of like your attention span." He thought he saw a trace of a smile play across her lips.

A few days later, Toby told Richard it was time for him to move off the cot in the office and find a place of his own. There was an apartment over the garage at Anna's house. Her widowed mother needed the income, and Toby needed his office back.

Anna helped him haul his few boxes up the stairs and introduced him to the idiosyncrasies of the flat: the switched hot and cold faucets in the shower, the hatchet handle that propped open the bedroom window on hot nights. He didn't say much in return. He tried not to stare but enjoyed watching her rock back slightly in her bare feet while she flipped through his vinyl albums, pausing every so often to study a cover.

That night she came to him like a shadow. She must have had an extra key. Through half-sleep he heard it scratch in the lock, heard her soft footsteps cross the floorboards, then a pause at the side of the bed as she shed her clothes, dropping them to the floor with a soft *whoomph*. She lifted the sheet and slipped in, wrapping herself around him in the warm dark.

He never knew why she came to him that first night, but she returned every night after, whether they worked the same shift or not, whether she spoke to him that day or not. She tasted of sorrow and a fierce hunger that thrilled him and burned his eyes with tears. He did not understand it, but he would not refuse it.

Gina woke up with a start. She pressed her tongue to the roof of her mouth and tried to work up some saliva to moisten it. Across from her, Richard slept, his head slumped to his chest. Down a few rows, a toddler couldn't settle. He strained against being held and slapped his hands against the window while his mother uttered a stream of admonitions: 'Stop it, be quiet, don't, give me that, don't touch, sit still, move your leg, leave that be.' The child answered with short wails and whines but no actual words. *I could do a better job than that,* Gina thought. She wouldn't harass the child who, at this young age, had already learned to stop listening to adults. *He'll be glad to get away from that as soon as he can.*

Outside, granite cliffs rose on either side of the train, creating a roofless tunnel. Suddenly, the rockface ended; they were sailing across a high bridge that floated over an expanse of gray fields and evergreen treetops. A sudden ache gripped her, a longing for flight. She sat up and pressed her forehead against the glass. New York and Lexi, her father, her mother's illness and death, the nuns and their condemnations, her old life trailed behind her like worn-out clothing that no longer fit. Here was the big, unfolding world. She could go anywhere she wanted. In the distance, the western horizon glowed with desert colors. The immensity of it took her breath away.

"Impressive, isn't it?"

She turned to Richard and saw a tired smile on his old face. "Is that where we're going?"

"No. Look there." He nodded to the north. She turned and saw an ominous force of dark clouds stationed over the hills. "We're headed straight for that."

11

Within a mile of their flight from Snyder, an easy silence settled between Anna and the boy. It was amazing how comfortable she felt, as if they had been traveling for days and this was just one more leg of a longer journey. She let up on the gas, and the car rocked them toward their destination.

When they arrived at the house, however, the mood shifted. The silence between them grew awkward and tense. After she parked beside a towering hemlock near the garage, she stood in the driveway confused, forgetting why she had brought him there. The boy waited with his hands jammed into the pockets of his hoodie and swayed back and forth slightly in his work boots. Overhead, dense clouds gathered. The air held itself, like an intake of breath.

Still giddy from the thrill of their escape, Anna gestured for the boy to follow her and resorted to chatter as she led him to the garden plot. "So, I thought, chicken wire. I'm sure I got the wrong things or not enough of the right things. I know that deer are a problem. And woodchucks. So, I tried to dig a trench. I didn't get very far. But then I thought, well, maybe I should get some of those things you stick into the ground, and they send off those sound waves that woodchucks hate? And of course, the only real way to keep the deer away is to put up an electrified fence, which I hate, but what do *I* know? It's probably the most effective way to go, but it just seems like such—what—overkill?"

The boy didn't say a word, not even those little reinforcing *uh-huh*s that keep a person going. His expression, half-obscured by the hood of his sweatshirt, was blank. It threw Anna. She didn't want to lose him. He was wild and wondrous, like a deer that had wandered into her kitchen. She forced herself to stop talking.

The boy walked the perimeter of the plot. "Nothing's ever simple," he mumbled, more to himself than to her. She wondered if he was lazy but dismissed the thought. It left behind, however, the realization that she knew practically nothing about this boy.

"These posts," he said finally, "they're too short to keep out the deer. And you don't have enough of them." His boot nudged the bale of chicken wire. "Where'd you get this?"

"From a shed behind the garage."

"Pretty rusty. Even new, this stuff is a bitch—sorry—hell—aw, shit. Jesus!" He covered his mouth to stop the avalanche of profanity.

Anna shook her head. "No. You're right. It is a bitch to work with."

He nodded and took a deep breath. "You don't really need a trench to keep the woodchucks out, just three feet of skirt."

"You mean a chicken wire skirt?"

"Yeah. They're pretty good diggers, but not three feet worth."

"I'm going to run out of chicken wire."

"Yeah."

"Do you think we have enough for the—what is it—skirt? Is there enough to dig down a little and lay the skirt in?"

The boy suppressed a smile. "Well, we can get started." He looked up. Anna followed his gaze. Purple clouds against the yellow sky reminded her of bruises that were slow to heal. In the distance, thunder growled. The boy shook his head. "Don't know how much time we'll have. Better get to it."

They worked together. The boy was surprisingly strong for someone so thin. He moved quickly and efficiently as he cut the sod into squares. Anna peeled them back while he severed any stubborn roots with the shovel. The tools that Anna bought were cheap, but they held. When they had finished digging out one of the longer sides of the plot, they laid a length of chicken wire into place and covered it with the squares of sod. In spare moments, Anna watched the boy.

There was a strangeness about him. Something not quite right. Despite his exertions, he kept his sweatshirt zipped up to his collarbone. He didn't even push up his sleeves. His only concession to the heat was to shake the hood off his head. As she watched him pick up a square of sod and throw it into position, she realized it was in the way he moved: conservatively, as if he was saving something for later. Then she saw it.

His arms. He kept them close to his body and used momentum to compensate for something his arms lacked: strength, range of motion, maybe even feeling. That gossip she had heard from the real estate agent and the woman in the diner resurfaced in her memory, something about someone's arms, something terrible. With sickening clarity, she realized: *he's the boy, the boy who fought off his mother's killer.* And then the rest of it: *this house was his grandfather's house, the house he lived in after his mother was killed.* She couldn't take her eyes off him as he stomped on the sod to urge the grass to take root again.

"You got any deer netting?" he said.

"Any what?"

"Comes in rolls. Black deer netting? For the fence? Since we're short on chicken wire?" He ran his hands through his dark hair, combing it back in rows that shone with sweat. Then, absentmindedly, he rubbed his hand up and down the length of his opposite arm, as if to soothe an ancient ache.

"Yes, I—I picked some up yesterday," Anna stammered. He

stopped rubbing his arm and gave her a sharp look. "I left it in the backseat of my car," she continued, in a small voice. "You want me to get it?"

He dropped his hand. His face reddened, and he pulled his hood back over his head.

"I'll go." He turned and walked with deliberate strides around the house and out of sight.

"Oh, God," Anna moaned. "God!" Her mind raced back to what the woman at the diner had told her.

He was only twelve, she'd said. In the heat of a summer's night, he and his mother had decided to sleep on the sunporch. Like a sleepover. A little adventure that she cooked up to distract him from the oppressive mugginess in the air. Maybe they slept on cots or on an inflatable mattress. She may have told him stories or hummed a song to ease him into sleep. Maybe she had set up a fan, something to stir the air. But the whir of it had masked the sounds of the intruder. Had some instinct awakened her and told her that something was not right? She would have gotten out of bed quietly, careful not to wake the boy. She would have walked cautiously through the dark rooms of the house to investigate. Maybe she called out and turned on the lights, or maybe she kept quiet, relying on cover of darkness and her familiarity with the house. Had she surprised the intruder, or had he been watching her from a dark corner all along, waiting for the best moment to strike?

There must have been a scuffle, sharp cries and muffled grunts that woke the boy, and when he found his mother missing, he must have come running toward those terrifying, unnatural sounds. He must have seen the man hitting her, pinning her against a wall or down onto the floor. Maybe the boy jumped onto the man's back and beat him with his small fists, and when he saw he was outweighed, he ran to the kitchen for a knife. Had the boy paused before using it? Had he hesitated to push the blade into the flesh of another? Was that his fatal mistake? Or had he charged forward like a wolf? Once the man had wrenched the knife from the boy's hand and turned it against him, the boy must have thrown up his arms to protect himself, with nothing between his skin and the blade on that terrible, hot night. And his mother...she must have done what Anna would have done and pushed herself between the man and her son. She took the blows and put up that futile struggle so her boy could run and save himself.

The gloom of the lead-colored sky bore down. A few large drops of rain fell, then more and more, gathering velocity. Within seconds a torrential downpour birthed small ponds in the grass and drenched Anna to the skin. Her hair whipped against her face as she ran toward the garage to find the boy.

Suddenly, the sky flashed bright white, and a deafening crack ripped the air. Then another sound, the resounding groan of wood splitting as the hemlock leaned and crashed onto her car. The roof crumpled, and the windshield burst into beads of glass as the car alarm blared.

Anna could not find the boy. She wiped the rain and hair from her face, but she couldn't see him anywhere. Another blast of lightning and an explosion of thunder jolted her. What if he was inside the car, trapped under that crush of metal and glass? She ran to the passenger side and crouched low, beating back sharp branches. She tried to pull the door open, but it was warped now and would not budge. A hand grabbed her arm and pulled her out of the thicket of branches as lightning seared the sky and thunder made the ground shiver. "C'mon!" The boy had her by the hand now. She couldn't believe he was real. She wrenched herself free and turned back to the car. He lunged for her wrist and dragged her across the driveway and up the steps to the porch, where he shoved the door open and pushed her inside.

Dripping and shivering, she stood before him. Outside, the car alarm shrieked.

The boy was pale, his eyes wide. "Lady..."

"I thought –" her knees buckled, and she grabbed his arm to steady herself. Once she found her balance, the boy gently twisted his arm from her grasp and backed away, holding up a hand to keep her at a distance.

"You okay?"

"Yeah," she panted. She closed her eyes and forced herself to slow her breathing. The sound of the car alarm cut through the air, reminding her that everything was not okay. A sob escaped her, then another. She put her hand over her mouth to stifle the rest.

"Jeeze, lady..."

Anna opened her eyes. She frightened him. Of course. He didn't know anything about her. To him, she was just some crazy, demanding, neurotic woman with no sense at all up from the city. "I'm sorry." She wiped her face with her hands and nodded toward his forehead. "You're bleeding. Must have been a branch. Come on. I'll fix that for you."

In the bathroom, she had him sit on the toilet seat and press a tissue to the cut while she searched the medicine cabinet for anti-septic and band-aids. "God. We don't have anything."

"It's okay."

"At least we can clean it with soap and water." She bent over him and pulled back the tissue. "The bleeding has stopped." She wet a washcloth and rubbed a bit of soap into it. "This might sting a little."

"It's *fine*." He took the washcloth from her, dabbed the wound and then stood to check it in the mirror. "I think I'll live." He turned and looked at her. "You might want to clean yourself up a bit."

She glanced at her reflection and saw a few scratches on her face and arms, marked by beads of red. As she wiped the blood away, she saw he was watching her. *God, he's tall. Taller than Ben, even.* Next to him, she felt shy, diminished. "Well. I'd better change my clothes." She started to leave and then turned back. "I'll see if I can dig up something for you."

"I'm fine."

"Stop saying that. You're not fine. You're a mess. You're all scratched up and drenched to the skin. You're covered with mud and pine needles. You can't stay in those wet clothes; you'll catch your death. Wash up while you're in here. Besides," she added, as if this was the final point that clinched her argument, "I don't want you tracking dirt all over the house."

In her bedroom, as she toweled off and changed into a pair of cotton drawstring pants and a gray pullover, she heard the shower running. Was it wise for him to do that? Wasn't there some old wives' tale about showering during a thunderstorm? It seemed so silly, so improbable, but it troubled her. Just as she was about to tell him to stop, the water cut off with a shuddering of old pipes and a final dribble, drip, drip.

She had searched for suitable clothing for the boy, but Richard's jeans were too short and way too big in the waist. Anna remembered she had something in the bottom drawer of her dresser, something of Ben's, an old Green Day t-shirt and a pair of jeans salvaged from his apartment.

She carried the clothes to the bathroom door and knocked. "I found something for you. Hand me your things. I'll do a quick load." The lock clicked and the door cracked open. A hand stuck out, holding a wad of heavy, wet clothes that Anna exchanged for dry.

After she got the wash started, she returned to the bathroom door. "Is everything okay?" It was so quiet in there. She knocked. "Hello?"

"I'm fine," he called. She waited for more. Finally, "I'll be out in a minute."

"Are you hungry?"

"Yeah. I could eat."

Anna smiled and went to the kitchen. From the window, she could see the car, its roof crushed under the hemlock. The rain still whipped about, but she didn't think any of the other trees were close enough to threaten the house. At least the thunder and lightning had backed off a bit.

For some reason, the car alarm had petered out. At some point, she should call the insurance company and let Richard know about the car. Her keys were still in there, along with her purse and her cellphone. She could never get a signal out here anyway. She picked up the house phone but heard only silence. It was then that she realized that she and the boy were marooned.

The refrigerator had little to offer: some eggs, an onion, butter. The contents of the cupboards weren't much better, but she could heat up a can of chicken noodle soup, finish off the sourdough. Comfort food. That's what this occasion called for. Scrambled eggs with sautéed onions, buttered toast, and a bowl of soup on the side. Bland on bland.

As she placed the onion on the cutting board, she heard the creak of the bathroom door and the soft thump of the boy's footsteps that stopped at the kitchen entrance. "Phone's dead," she said, keeping her back to him. Silence. She turned to look, holding the knife poised mid-air over the chopping block.

His hair was a mass of wet curls that darkened the shoulders of the t-shirt. Hanging from the short sleeves were his arms: pale, limp, thatched with scars that climbed from his hands to above his elbows. Anna's eyes found his face. It was as blank as a concrete wall. She swallowed and tried a light tone, as if by sheer force of attitude, she could move them to a normal plane. "I hope you like eggs."

She turned back to her work, but he wasn't having any of it. He crossed to her side and flopped his forearms onto the counter next to the cutting board, leaning on his elbows. "Need any help?" A dare, with no help in sight. Anna rested the knife on the wooden block and forced herself to look more closely at his arms.

The damage was horrific. The scoring, erratic and frenzied, cut deep. In some places, it must have gotten close to the bone. She wanted to touch, to stroke, to lay her hands on the long-held pain. But motherly comfort had no purchase here. In the history of the world, all the murmured *there-theres* and *it's okays* would fall silent, meaningless on these arms. So, she looked into his eyes instead, and there they were: Ben's eyes, dark, wide open, willful and on a search of their own.

"Yes," she said quietly, handing him the knife. "Dice the onion, will you?"

12

Rain pounded the asphalt and flooded the tracks. There was no building at the train depot in the port town, only a sheltered bench flanking the parking lot. Gina was the first to dash from the train to the shelter, shrieking as she ran. "C'mon!" she called, shaking the water from her hair.

Richard tightened his grip on his bag and winced as he stepped down to the concrete walkway. He couldn't run. His knees wouldn't allow it, but he hurried his steps as he tucked his head and squinted against the downpour.

There was no sign of Anna or the Audi in the parking lot, still no message on Gina's cell. He sank onto the bench and dialed the house's landline. A recorded voice told him that the number he had reached was not available for service.

"God. What a wasteland." Gina surveyed the parking lot. "Nothing. Not even cabs."

A fast food restaurant across the street glowed, a garish oasis.

"Let's head over there. We can warm up while I try to get hold of Anna."

"Whatever you say, boss."

Inside, they ordered coffee and sat a few tables away from the only other customer, an old-timer hunched over a Styrofoam cup.

"Why is it that all these fast-food joints are this sickening bright yellow and red? It's so jarring." Gina sprinkled sugar into her coffee.

Richard continued to fiddle with the cellphone. "I don't

know...yes, I do. It's supposed to stimulate appetite. You see them on snack food wrappers: red, yellow, orange, sometimes brown. Warm colors. Happy. Cheerful. Makes people want to eat."

"Oh, yeah. I forgot. Your line of work."

"Yours, too."

"Not anymore."

"No." Richard returned his attention to the phone. "Not anymore."

Gina watched him stab the keys with his finger. "You know what they say about insanity."

"I don't understand it. I can't get anything. Not her cell, not the landline. I can't even leave a message."

"Could she be on her way here?"

"I called from the train and left a voicemail with our arrival time, but you'd think she would call back and let me know she was coming." Richard hung up and looked out the window. The streetlamps came on, casting a vaporous, orange glow over the parking lot.

"If she's comin' from up north, ain't nobody getting through on Route 97."

Richard turned to the other customer. "What was that?"

The old man spoke into his coffee. "State trooper was in a while ago. Said 97 was closed. Power's out in most of the county up north. Big winds. Lotta downed trees and wires."

"Did he say when the road might be cleared?"

The old man looked at the ceiling and ruminated. "He said crews'll be working through the night. Said it might be clear sometime tomorrow."

Richard sighed. "This day just keeps on giving."

"Are there any hotels around here?" Gina smiled at the man. "Close enough to walk to?"

The man let out a long, ragged breath. "Well, there was the Excelsior. That shut down last year. The Delaware ain't far. Just got fixed up."

"Where is that?"

"Few blocks down on South Main. Can't miss it. Big red building. Used to be the old train depot. There's a tiki bar next door."

"All right, then," Gina grinned at Richard.

They were soaked to the skin by the time they walked into the hotel lobby. The manager, a lean, sad-faced man who looked as if the life had been bleached out of him, was afraid he couldn't offer them a room. The hotel wouldn't officially open until next week, if they wanted to come back then. The tiki bar was taking customers, if they felt like getting a bite.

Richard turned to Gina. "Give me your wallet." She raised an eyebrow but handed it to him. He rifled through its folds and pulled out a fifty. "You've probably got at least one room that's a little more ready than the others."

The manager pressed his lips together as if his teeth ached. "I might. It would be in the basement."

Richard put the fifty on the counter. "Perfect. We won't be any trouble. How much?"

"We're not really open, you understand. The painters are still working on the hallway down there, so you'd have to watch out for ladders and drop clothes and whatnot...but the room is made up. You'd have plenty of privacy and all..." At this, his eyes flicked to Gina. "The going rate would be...two hundred."

Gina stared at him and then turned to Richard. "Let's go."

A head of wild white-blond hair popped up from behind the counter, a child with piercing blue eyes set against olive skin. Gina's gaze rested on her. The man turned toward the child and spoke in soft tones, "Sunny. Go on back in. I'll be there in a minute." The child's wide eyes set on Gina, and she pointed a short finger at her as if casting a diminutive spell. Transfixed, all three adults watched her hold Gina's gaze, then turn and retreat to a back room that pulsed with the light and sound of a television.

The manager turned back to Gina and Richard. "Because it's in the basement, we're down to one-fifty?"

"We'll give you a hundred. Cash," Gina said, laying another fifty on the counter. Richard opened his mouth, then shut it again. "And we need to get out of these wet clothes," she continued. "Do you have a couple of bathrobes?"

"As I said, we're pretty no-frills here right now," the manager said, sliding the money from the counter and tucking it into his pocket. "But I guess we could find a couple of robes. You're next to the laundry. Feel free to use the machines."

Richard had been in so many hotel rooms in his life that they blurred together, like passing strip malls. This room was no different from any other with its innocuous art, its mauve, teal, and gray color scheme, endless chatter from the television. Yet, as he sat on the edge of his bed, he knew that however long he lived, he would never forget this room. It was fitting that he should find himself in a place that attempted and failed to create an illusion of luxury. Exposed copper pipes ran the length of the low ceiling. The windows, placed just above their heads, looked out at the sidewalk and would have revealed the footsteps of pedestrians, had pedestrians existed in this ghost town.

Gina passed in and out of the room as she tended the laundry. Through the open door, he could hear the faint, rhythmic thump of their clothes in the dryer and the occasional release of virgin cubes into the ice machine farther down the hall.

"You're lucky," Gina said as she unpacked his bag. "You have a change of clothes." She placed his pullover, underwear and socks in a dresser drawer as if they were planning to stay for a week. "I don't have a choice. Hell, I don't even have a toothbrush. But you—you sure you want to wear the stuff that's in the dryer? You don't want to put these on?" She held up a clean pair of khakis. When she got no reply, she shrugged and crossed to the closet, catching a glimpse of herself in the full-length mirror. "God, I hate bathrobes. They make me look so middle-aged. No offense." She draped his pants over the bar of a wooden hanger. "What do you want to do for dinner?"

"You're like a bird," he said, eyes fixed on the cellphone in his hand.

She turned to him. "A what?"

"A bird. Building a nest. You never stop moving." His gaze drifted to his legs, poking from beneath the hem of his robe. When had they become hairless, like his father's in his old age?

"I'm not moving now," she said.

"Well, *now*."

"The clothes will be ready soon. Let's get dinner. I'm starving. Besides, I want to see this so-called 'tiki bar.'" A silence lengthened between them. "Hey. Don't you think it's about time you snapped out of it?"

Richard sighed and pushed himself up from the bed. "Snap. I'm taking a shower."

"We'll start with an order of fried calamari. Two plates, please. And then I'll have the Delaware Deluxe Burger and a Coke." Gina handed her menu to the waiter. "Richard?" She tapped the back of his menu. "Richard."

He blinked. "What? Yeah. I'll have the meatloaf, I guess. And a scotch straight up. Make it a double."

"Is there any special –?"

"The house scotch will do."

"You know what?" Gina tapped the waiter's arm. "Scratch the Coke. I'll have a beer. Pick something interesting. Not too hoppy." Gina smiled at Richard as the waiter retreated. "Why not? Let's get this party started."

Richard breathed a mirthless laugh.

Gina leaned her elbows on the table and looked around the dining room. "Lots of palm fronds in here. And ukuleles. Bamboo. Hula skirts. Oh, look! Over the bar...a surfboard with a shark bite in it. I hope you're appreciating the décor. Someone put a lot of thought into this place."

"Someone with a Hawaiian hangover."

"Listen to you. You made a joke."

"I'm trying."

He looked like he was about to cry. She wasn't good with wallowers. Never had been. It wasn't like someone had died. He'd get another job, maybe even a better one. It's not like he just lost his job *and* his home *and* his wife was some junkie who was laid out on a filthy mattress in a burnt-out shell of a building with her pusher lying next to her. It's not like his whole fucking life was ripped to shreds. Gina managed to put on a smile when the waiter delivered their drinks. "Will you look at how the place has filled up? Who knew this many people even lived here?"

Richard knocked his scotch back and tapped the table for another. "Lucky us. We finally found the center of the universe."

"Maybe we did. Or maybe the universe is so vast, so infinite, so...unfixed that there is no true center. Maybe *every* spot in the universe is its center. Maybe the universe is nothing *but* centers."

"*Okay*. Okay." Richard pulled the cellphone out of his pocket.

"Put that thing away."

"But I have to check –"

"She'll call. Now put it away. Or give it back to me. You're eating dinner, for chrissakes." Richard gave her a weak smile but held onto the phone. "Anyway..." she scanned the room.

Lexi would have had a field day with this place. She would have drunk too much and mocked the well-scrubbed waiters and grabbed one of the ukuleles off the wall, laughing the whole time as she sang and twirled until she spun out and crashed into the salad bar, making one of her classic messes that she'd leave for someone else to clean up. God. In a few months, Gina would probably wonder how she'd ever gotten herself tangled up with such a lunatic. But tonight, she missed Lexi, missed the drug that Lexi was. Missed the storm of Lexi's life that had swirled around Gina as she tried to maintain her footing. She sighed and nodded at Richard. "So, what's the plan for tomorrow?"

"I don't know. Get hold of Anna. If I can't do that, we'll grab a cab as soon as the roads clear."

Gina couldn't see it. She couldn't see herself at the happy reunion between Richard and his wife. It just didn't feel right. For the last twenty-four hours she'd managed to live in the moment as if she were surfing an earthquake, just barely staying on top as she rode catastrophic shifts. But now as she cast her mind forward, she saw herself in motion, always in motion, until finally, she stood still and looked at a view of blue—ocean or sky, she couldn't tell, maybe both—but it felt like home.

They sat out the rest of the meal in silence. By the time their plates were cleared, a small group of musicians had arrived and were setting up to play on a raised platform at one end of the bar.

"Huh. Look who it is." Gina nodded toward the stage.

The manager from the hotel pulled a guitar out of its case and began tuning up with the rest of the band. The little girl—his daughter, Gina supposed—was camped at a small table just below the apron of the stage. She was dressed in pajamas now and wore slippers with ducks crowning the toes. Beside her chair, a little red suitcase yawned open on the floor. From it she pulled a yellow blanket that she draped over the table. Then she sat a teddy bear on the blanket so that it faced the stage. She surrounded the toy with articles of clothing: t-shirts, scarves, underwear, emptying the entire suitcase to provide a cozy nest for her bear. When she'd set it up just right, she whispered into the bear's ear and laid her head on the table, encircling him with her arms. *What a little mother*, Gina thought, surprised at the ache in her throat.

As the hotel-clerk-father-now-musician picked a gentle lilting tune on his guitar and sang of a moment captured in a lost photograph, the child's small fingers tapped a light rhythm on the tabletop, then slowed and stopped as sleep overcame her.

The band played and the crowd quieted for them. Deep into the set, the lights dimmed slightly, and a woman appeared on stage. Her dark, curly hair framed her face and fell to her shoulders. She wore a tank top, a beaded gauze skirt, and boots. Her skin held a darker, richer olive tone than the child's. Quietly, she stepped up to the microphone and looked at the child's father, who held her gaze. In one voice, they sang:

I been calling you,
I been calling you,
I been calling you in from the rain.

As their voices split off, rising and falling in harmony and dissonance, they sang of a splintered love that could not be mended. The last note hung in the air unresolved. Then the woman stepped off the apron and quietly packed the child's clothes and the teddy bear into the suitcase while the man strummed a low refrain on his guitar. Careful not to wake her, the woman gathered her girl into her arms. In her sleep, the child wrinkled her face as she wrapped her legs around her mother's waist and aligned herself with her body. With these burdens in hand—suitcase and child— the woman slowly made her way toward the exit of the bar. When Gina turned to follow her departure, she saw that Richard was staring at the empty space left by the child. His face had lost its shape and glistened with tears. A strange, low moan escaped his lips. The sound grew louder and rose in pitch.

"Richard." Gina stood and touched his shoulder. He turned his face to hers, and she saw him as a child, distressed, uncomprehending. He opened his mouth wide and wailed and did not stop as she got him to his feet and led him by the arm to the door.

13

The last thing you want to do is chop onions, but your instincts kick in, and you take the knife from her anyway. Lessons from the street are hard to shed, even in this kitchen that you know so well with this stranger of a woman who is the color of stones. The street taught you: if you show fear or weakness, you die. And a knife, yes, a knife is a weapon, sharp and sure, but it is also a prop. It tells the world who you are: a badass who should not be fucked with.

It's been a long time since you held a knife. Your hand twitches a little, but she doesn't notice. She moves away and turns her back to you—a stupid move—and starts messing with a can of something and a pot. The knife has more heft than you expected, good blade, long tang. You curl your fingers around the handle, easing its contours into your palm and find its balance. It feels like...power. You pivot your body so you can always see her out of the corner of your eye. That wall behind you is a problem. It denies you an escape route, but it also guarantees nothing's going to sneak up behind you. Just one angle to worry about. And then, you've got the knife.

Rain drums the roof. Wind rumbles the eaves. Your eyes flick to the window and see that the downed tree and crumpled car have melted into the darkness, silent now that the car alarm has stopped screaming.

It's strange to be in this kitchen. There are traces of your grandfather here, of your mother, of your child-self. You are here now but you are also peering through a window of time. Your old, dimly remembered life suddenly feels so close you could almost touch it. But you are no longer part of the world that was filled with the sound of your mother humming as she stood at the stove, stirring applesauce and filling the air with the scent of cinnamon and cloves or the clamor of your grandfather stomping caked-on dirt from his boots in the mudroom.

What was it that Phoenix said in that slow way of his? Everything we experience is in the past: "Even what you're saying right now is in the past. As soon as your mind has pulled a thought together, formed it into words, as soon as those words leave your lips, milliseconds have rushed by. It's all past. And kid, when you spend too much time in the past, you abandon the present."

Thoughts of Phoenix, of his little wisdoms, prick your eyes. Your friend and sometimes companion on the streets. Your kinship: you, with your scars; he, with his burns and missing arm after an IED in Iraq relieved him of his duty. And then that morning. A fire in the abandoned warehouse, other squatters shouting, gunfire. He told you to run. Told you he was right behind you. Until he wasn't.

There's a tight little knot in your gut: nerves. You're not crazy about nerves. Things go wrong with nerves. Back in the bathroom, your old fear of helplessness fed a surge of panic. You almost climbed out the window. And now your lungs are catching again; the knot in your gut stiffens. You must calm down. You force a long, quiet sigh— one of those 'cleansing breaths' that Phoenix used to go on about when you were camped in the park and either cops or—worse, marauders— raged through the night. As air leaves your body, the knot loosens a little.

"Focus on the now, kid."

"Yeah, but what if the 'now' is really shitty?" you always whispered, and he would shake his head and laugh.

"Like I said, kid. It's already past."

You trim the ends off the onion and peel away the papery skin. The blade makes a shushing sound as you rock it through the onion's

*meat. Invisible gas stings your eyes; the diced fragments, white gems,
gleam.*

*It's nice when the lady doesn't talk. She's all business now, crack-
ing eggs into a bowl and jiggling a little when she beats them with a
fork. A pat of butter sizzles in the frying pan. She turns to you, smiling
and holds out her hand. She nods at the cutting board, and you realize she doesn't fear you. She trusts you. She takes the cutting board,
dumps the onion gems into the pan, and lets them sizzle before she
pushes them around with a wooden spoon. The aroma sends a sudden
wave of nostalgia washing over you. It surprises you and bothers you,
but you don't want it to go away. You stay very still, very quiet, very
hidden in silence the way Phoenix taught you so you can see but not
be seen.*

They sat at the kitchen table next to the window. The boy ate
overhand, holding his spoon in his fist. Anna looked out the window at the expanse of black. In the reflection, she saw the boy put
down his spoon, pick up the soup bowl with both hands, and drink
the remains. He ignored the paper napkins she'd set out and used
the collar of his t-shirt—Ben's t-shirt—to wipe his mouth. Then
he folded his hands in his lap, slumped in his chair, and stared at
his empty plate.

She turned from the window to the light of the kitchen. "Can
I get you anything else? I could scramble more eggs."

"No. I'm good. Thanks."

"I'm not going to be able to get you home tonight."

"I could always walk."

"That's ridiculous. I wouldn't let you. It's a mess out there."
The boy said nothing. Anna opened her mouth, then stopped herself. Finally, "You know, it's not your fault."

"What?"

"Your father. The way he spoke to you. The things he said to you. That's...rough."

The boy shrugged.

"You mustn't think that any of it is true."

He stared at her; his expression unreadable. "How do you know it's not true?"

"What I mean is –"

"No, really, how do you know? Maybe he's right. Maybe I'm the biggest fuck-up in the world. It's possible, you know."

"You mustn't feel –"

"Lady –"

"You're just a child –"

"But I'm not. You act like you know me. You don't. You don't know anything about me. Stop thinking you do."

She started to speak, but suddenly the lights pulsed and died. The refrigerator stopped humming, and the furnace broke off a low whistle that she hadn't noticed before. All was darkness and silence, except for the rain and wind hitting the house in percussive bursts.

"Dammit," she said. "And me with no candles in the freezer."

Silence falls like death, complete silence in the moments after the world goes dark. It is a darkness that the eye can't pierce. As much as you might look for the smallest flicker of light, the tiniest beacon, you remain blind, rudderless in the dark. It is the darkness of that night. The night the world ended. You begin to feel that old panic, a want of air and light. From the depths, your mind swims for the surface, calling on all your senses to give you some clue, some bearing. Then a voice like your mother's—a lifeline—says something about candles, and you grab hold of it: light in the form of sound.

Soon, other sounds, natural sounds speak: wind whistles and

wails and finds passage through the cracks and chinks in the old house.
You imagine yourself as a passenger on the wind's back. It brings you
to a sense of place. You are at the kitchen table. You just ate toast and
eggs from a plate. You drank soup from a bowl. You are here.

The lady doesn't have much on hand for emergencies, not even
a flashlight. She does have a box of kitchen matches. You feel around
in one of the drawers in the mudroom where candles have been kept
forever, since your mother was a girl and sure enough, a few decent
stubs roll around in the back. The lady dumps the dishes into the sink
and follows you to the living room with a lit candle in each hand. She
asks if you could build a fire, so you do.

The way she watches you is a little weird. It's so close, as if she's
afraid she might miss something. Like she's looking for something. She
moves the candles to shed as much light as possible on your hands,
wherever they go. And still, she's quiet. She doesn't pester you with
a lot of annoying questions. Finally, you realize, she's learning. She
doesn't know what you know. But she wants to.

The boy was a wizard. In a few short minutes, he did what she
could not: provide heat and light. She saw now how it worked.
He started with wads of newspaper as she had the night before,
gathering them into a nest under the grate. He worked artfully, like
a craftsman. From a wooden box next to the fireplace, he pulled
some kindling and laid it on the grate in a crisscrossed pattern.
On top of that he continued the pattern with larger sticks, then
another layer of still larger sticks, and finally four logs of split
wood on top. When he lit the newspaper, she saw the structure as a
beautiful little oven that bloomed with light as the flames climbed
through the wood, brightening each layer. "I think we should sleep
down here, in front of the fireplace," she said.

"Why?"

"It just seems safer. In case a tree falls on the house. Or in case something else happens."

"Like what?"

"I don't know…a fire. Wild animals. Nuclear holocaust. Who knows? The point is, we'd be in the same room, and we could help each other."

He shrugged. "Fine."

"Fine," she repeated. "Dibs on the sofa."

While she's upstairs getting blankets, you do the secret thing. The important thing. The thing that will get you through the night. You sneak into the kitchen, wiped off the knife, and take it with you to the living room. You figure you'll sleep on the floor in front of the fireplace, so you slip the knife under the rug bordering the hearth.

So, there.

There, now.

Funny how calm you feel, even with the lights out. The knife puts you on home turf. Now you're the one in charge.

Anna didn't waste time pawing through the linen closet. Instead, she simply pulled the blankets off her bed and folded them as best as she could in the dark. Before she left her room, she stopped herself. The box. It was his. She felt for the closet door and opened it. As her hand ran along the shelf, it lingered a moment over Ben's box of ashes. Then it traveled on and grasped the handle of the tackle box. She pulled it down and tucked it under the pile of blankets. She wouldn't give it to him right away. Not yet. She would wait for the right moment. It would be a shock for him. But the important thing was that it was his.

"So, who's the hunter?"

You are lying on your back in a nest of quilts and pillows. The lady sits on the sofa with her feet tucked under her. Flames crackle and firelight glints off the glass eyes of the taxidermy. The stuffed owl on the rafter—the one with the squirrel clutched in its talons—stares down at you. Its outstretched wings cast shadows on the ceiling. The knife resting under the rug presses against your thigh.

"I mean that moose, for instance," she says. "What's the story there?"

So. She expects you to chit-chat like a normal person. Okay. Sure. You can play that game. "That moose head is about sixty years old," you tell her. "My grandfather shot him at the lake."

"I didn't know moose came this far south."

"They don't, usually."

"How often?"

"Once every sixty years." You smile. A little joke. You didn't know you had it in you.

"What about that owl and squirrel?"

"We were out early one morning. Right at daybreak. I shot the squirrel and before I could pick it up, an owl swooped down to grab it, so my grandfather shot it, too."

"Sounds like a character, your grandfather."

"Well, he liked to shoot things."

"Did he shoot all of these? Except for your squirrel?"

"Uh-huh."

"Do you like to shoot things?"

What the fuck was that supposed to mean? You pivot. "So, who's the Green Day fan?"

An abrupt stillness comes over her, like a deer that senses danger. And you, too, grow still, a coyote catching its scent.

She draws a deep breath. "That shirt was my son's."

A tension gathers in the circle of firelight, and one of the burning logs emits a high-pitched hum. A spark shoots against the fire screen, *and logs shift and resettle gently into a new arrangement of embers and flame. You ask the question even though you're pretty sure you know the answer.* "Why do you have it?"

It takes her a few beats to answer. "He was killed last year. Shot in a mugging. They never caught the guy. There were no witnesses."

"So, how do you know it was a guy?"

If it had been anyone else, Anna would have ended the conversation and turned her back on him. But this boy had a history that allowed her to forgive. And he had a point. In all her imaginings of that night, it never occurred to her that Ben's killer could have been female. In fact, even as a male, the face of the killer did not exist for her. He was a shrouded figure, shadowy and evanescent. In her darkest dreams, he was a being apart from life, a shapeshifter, Mr. Death himself who stepped into the stream of life to divert it and stepped out again to leave the living engulfed in floodwaters of horror and heartbreak.

"It never goes away," she whispered, giving voice to a private thought. "This feeling of being in the depths. I can't pull out of it. I live a shadow-life. Nothing matters, and I don't understand why I'm still here."

"It could be worse."

"How could it be worse?"

"It could be your fault."

The dream is back. It steals up on you in your sleep like a panther. Everything is slow: the sweep of the blade. The slump of her body against the wall. The wave of your arms, like seaweed in dark water. A death dance. No words. Just grunts and gasps and high-pitched cries. Then your mother's last word to you, whispered. Her cheek rests on the hardwood floor. Her eyes stare across the boards: "Run."

You should stay. You should be with her as she slips away. You think you have time, but time has shifted. You are in a whole new universe of time. What takes forever is over in a moment, and what takes a moment lasts forever.

She woke to the sounds of whimpers and cries that reminded her of her childhood dog who sometimes yelped and twitched in his sleep, dreaming perhaps of a squirrel that got away.

Anna sat up and through bleary eyes saw the fireplace with glowing embers that cast a faint, red light across the floor. Below her was someone in the throes of a nightmare.

Ben?

No.

Not Ben.

Someone else.

The boy.

His back was to her, and he twisted and moaned words without meaning. She knelt beside him and watched him for a bit, not sure of the best way to wake him. A thought struck her; its absurdity almost made her laugh: she didn't know his name.

"Hey," she whispered. She put her hand on his shoulder. He shouted and jerked away. His eyes were wild as he bolted upright and stared at her, not seeing her at all. She grabbed him more firmly to give him a good shake, and suddenly, she saw a flash of red firelight between them. He was brandishing it, warning her away with it. Then she saw it for what it was: a knife. What a fool she had been.

14

Richard's wails grew louder as they stepped out of the tiki bar. A driving rain pounded the sidewalk. Gina led Richard under a storefront awning, but he broke free and lurched to the middle of the empty street. There he stood with his face turned to the night sky as he howled indecipherable words. Then he paused, as if waiting for a reply. When none came, he sank to his knees and hung his head.

From under the awning, Gina watched as dark raindrops bounced off his back. What was she supposed to do with this guy, this old guy who had run out of rope? Who broke down at the sight of a child in her mother's arms? Gina was hanging onto the thinnest shred of hope herself. She was drained of care for anyone else. So, she waited and let Richard cry. It wasn't until she noticed approaching headlights in the distance that she went to him. "Come on, Richard. Time to go."

"No." He slumped onto his side and lay there with his knees pulled up to his chest.

"Richard. I'm not kidding. There's a car coming."

"No."

The headlights loomed larger. In desperation, she gave his thigh a sharp kick. "Cut the crap! You're going to get us both killed." She grabbed his arm as he struggled to his feet. The blare of the car's horn spurred him to the curb. When he tried to sit, she hauled him back to his feet. "Nope. Come on. Time to dry off."

Back in the hotel, Gina led Richard to the bathroom. For the second time in the last twenty-four hours, she stripped off his clothes and left them in a wet heap on the floor. Richard stood silent and naked, his old man's body with its sad folds of flesh and graying hair swayed slightly as he stared at the tiled wall while Gina filled the tub. She eased him into the steaming water and lathered up a washcloth. Washing him, she found, calmed her.

Afterward, he sat in his robe on the side of the bed and stared at the high, dark window that looked out at the sidewalk. "Richard?" Nothing. "I'm putting our clothes in the dryer. Then I'm going to take a quick shower." Still nothing. "Anyway. I'll be right here. If you need me."

How good it felt to stand under the hot water. To feel it wash down her body and sluice off the sorrow of this man, the sadness of the broken family in the tiki bar, the refuse of last night and of so many nights before that. Another cleansing. Another fresh start.

When she emerged from the bathroom, wearing a robe and toweling off her hair, she saw that Richard was right where she had left him, sitting on the edge of the bed, staring into space.

"Richard. Let's go to sleep now. It's been a long, rough day. My mother always used to say, 'Nighttime is no time to solve –"

"I never told her," Richard cut in, eyes still fixed ahead of him.

"What?"

"I never told her."

"Never told who what?

"I never told Anna what I know. What I know about her, and what I know about Ben."

"Richard. I don't understa–"

"I'm sterile," he said. "I found out years ago, about six months after Ben was born. We'd decided that we didn't want any more children, so I went in for a vasectomy. Turns out I'd been shooting blanks the whole time."

"So, that means –"

"Yes."

"Do you know who –?"

"I've got a pretty good idea. An old friend. I heard he died a few years ago. Liver cancer." His tone was wistful, defeated. He cocked his head slightly to one side, as if he were straining to hear a scrap of music.

As she watched him, the full meaning of his revelation sank in, the burden of the secret he carried. Wasn't this what life was all about, this peeling back of layers that revealed wounds that would never heal? Or if they did, they healed incompletely, leaving shadow wounds behind. Life turned on these wounds. They traveled with us, drove us in unexpected directions.

Everyone has a story. And she, she now realized, was a collector of stories. She listened to them, held them close and took care of them. This was her work in the world. And as a collector of stories, she embraced the fact that people are flawed. They live complicated lives filled with joy and sorrow, courage and terror. Quietly, she sat next to Richard and cocked her head to one side, listening for what he listened for.

After a length of silence, he spoke. "I never said a word. She was so in love with Ben. I just couldn't tell her that I knew. Everything would have fallen apart. Everything. So, I pretended. Because she needed this one thing that I couldn't give her. I thought I was big enough to make it not matter. But whenever I looked at Ben, I never saw myself there. I questioned everything about him. Every time he screwed up, every time he hurt me or disappointed me, I told myself it was because he wasn't mine." Here Richard stopped and drew a jagged breath. "But he *was* mine. DNA doesn't matter. He was entrusted to me. It wasn't my job to find myself in him. It was my job to learn who he was."

Gina let silence rest between them. Gently, she took his hand. "You missed the mark."

"The what?"

"One of the nuns at my old school used to say that a sin is when you miss the mark. In her gym class, whenever you'd shoot for the basket and miss, she'd say, 'Oh, that's a sin.' I kind of liked that. I took it to mean that there's always another chance. To try again and maybe, this time, hit the mark."

"Not for me."

"If you try –"

"It's too late."

"If I were your son, and you tried, knowing what you know –"

"You don't understand." He turned his face to her, and she saw it: utter hopelessness and loss. The despair of the irreversible. "He's gone. He's never coming back. There will be no second chances."

15

You are in the mist again. It blankets the forest floor, hiding a tangle of roots and fallen limbs. You try to obey her whispered command; you try to run. But as always, the mist rises and thickens until there is nothing but mist. It clings to you, insists that you surrender to gravity, to the grave that opens up for you. You want to fight. You want to resist the ground's desire to pull you into the great silence. You open your mouth to cry for help, but your voice has abandoned you. You raise your knife even though you know it is useless against the mist, against ghosts with their unyielding invitations. Just as you are about to strike, a voice pierces the mist. For the first time in this dream, you hear her. She is singing a long-ago song from long-ago bedtimes when she laid next to you and ran her hand along your back to lull you to sleep. Her voice is so close its vibrations pierce your heart, and you lean in, straining to hear. Like a night bird, you sing your own muted song: she is here, she is here, she is here.

The moment the blade rises between them, flashing orange and red in the firelight, a strange calm envelopes Anna. *So, this is how death comes,* she thinks. She sinks onto her heels and lowers her eyes.

Let it come.

As she waits, a simple scratch of music and a crawl of words come to her. They wind through her like an unspoken wish. She opens her mouth to let them out. The tune, weak and hesitant, is so familiar. Something from long ago. Something she sang to Ben in the dark. He loved it because it had a bird in it. She loved it because it spoke of loss and homecoming.

Make my bed and light the light,
I'll be coming home tonight
Black bird
Bye –

A clatter of metal on stone interrupts her. Reluctantly, she looks at him. The boy, awake now, stares at her with haunted eyes. The fading fire illuminates the contours of one side of his face, leaving the other side in shadow. In this light, his features seem even more finely drawn, even the tiny wrinkles that gather between his eyebrows and at the corners of his mouth.

Slowly, she reaches her hand out and rests it on his chest. Through Ben's t-shirt, she feels a heartbeat, fast and strong. She closes her eyes.

I miss you.
I miss you.
I miss you.
I do.

When she opens her eyes, her vision clears. She sees the boy for who he is, and he sees her for who she is. She pulls her hand back and reaches for the tackle box in its hiding place under the sofa. "I think this is yours," she says, placing it at his knees.

A whispered gasp escapes him as he rests his hands on the lid. He looks at Anna. "It was my grandfather's."

"Now it's yours." Anna picks up the knife from the floor and stands. "You won't need this tonight."

She walks the knife back to the kitchen, leaving him alone with the box. When she returns, the boy is lying on his side, facing the last of the firelight. His eyes are closed, and he hugs the box to his chest as he would a lover. In his hand he holds the letter from his mother.

Saturday

16

The parking lot at the train station was dotted with pools of rainwater reflecting a pale blue sky. Richard picked his way around them, surprised to see so few cars, even at this early hour. Where were the commuters? Weren't people expected to be somewhere? He paused near a cement bench and took a seat. Of course. The weekend.

The clean, newly-washed air promised a glorious day—clear and brilliant—full of possibilities. *I am a free man.* It was true. He felt raw as a newborn. He felt hopeful for no good reason.

Back at the hotel, he'd managed to slip out of bed, dress, and pack without waking Gina. She lay on her side, wrapped in the hotel's white robe. A strand of pink and black hair draped across her cheek, and her eyelids twitched with sleep. When Richard gently pulled the hair off her face, she panted once and then settled back into her dream world. Before he left, Richard sat at the desk to write a note. When he finished, he folded it neatly, wrote her name on the outside and placed it next to her pillow. His last act was to kiss his fingertips and touch the top of her head.

A collection of utility trucks huddled at one side of the parking lot, their engines emitting low rumbles, as if impatient to get on with the job. A road crew stood nearby, drinking coffee. Richard approached them. "Do you know how the roads look heading north?"

One of the workers, a sinewy, sun-cured woman who was enjoying a cigarette with her coffee shook her head. "Route 97 is open, but I don't know about the backroads. Lotta trees down. Wires, too. They're bringing in crews from out of state, but there's no telling when the power will be back."

Of course. Now it made sense. Anna couldn't possibly have gotten his messages on the landline. And her cell probably ran out of juice. *Just a little power outage,* he comforted himself.

"You headed up there?" he asked the woman.

"Right after breakfast," she said, blowing a puff of smoke out of the side of her mouth.

"I don't suppose you could give me a lift? I'm trying to get to my wife. I haven't been able to get through to her on the phone."

"Nah. We couldn't. Against regulations." She nodded at a rust-eaten pickup truck parked about fifty feet away. "You might try Brady over there. He's headed up-county with his chainsaw."

Brady, who looked like he'd barely broken into his twenties, was happy to have company. "Just give me a second to clear some space," he said as he moved a lunch bag and thermos from the passenger seat.

Richard climbed in, enjoying with boyish delight the height of the truck. It was surprisingly neat and clean inside the cab. On the driver's visor, he noticed a snapshot of a young woman holding a toddler, both smiling at the camera. There was something off about the child, a flattened face and almond-shaped eyes that slanted upward. A word from Richard's childhood came to mind, one that his parents forbade him to use, even though the kids on the playground tossed it around with cruel glee. "Nice family," he said.

Brady glanced at the photo and smiled. "Thanks. That's my home crew. My reason for living."

As they drove along the winding road that overlooked the river, Brady kept up a steady stream of chatter. It wasn't long before

Richard knew all about how Brady and Tiffany had met at church, how she was a few years older than he, but it didn't seem to matter too much, and how the child was hers from a previous relationship with a real screw-up, but let's not be too harsh because we're all flawed and blessed in God's eyes. Besides, Brady figured he'd gotten a package deal with the kid thrown in for free.

Richard, to his surprise, enjoyed hearing about Brady's life. It was a window into a whole other reality. It would be tough for Brady and his family. Richard could see the challenges that lay ahead for this young man, even if Brady couldn't see them for himself. Two days ago, Richard would have found his youthful optimism naive. But on this morning, Richard admired Brady and his insistence that life was 'all good.'

Up ahead, the road shrank to one lane as exhausted night crews directed traffic around the remaining debris. Once they passed, Richard turned his attention to the view, an expansive, breathtaking sight with forested mountains towering over the river.

At the turn heading north, Brady pulled over at the entrance of a new housing development.

"I gotta drop you off here," he said. "I'm headed west. There'll be a bit of traffic running north. It may take a little while, but you should be able to hitch a ride."

"Can I give you something for your trouble?" Richard reached for his pocket, forgetting that he had no wallet, no money. It was strange not to be able to pay for a favor.

"No trouble at all," said Brady. "I was headed up here anyway. It was nice to have company."

Richard thanked him, wished him well, and dismounted the truck. After he waved Brady off, he turned toward the development.

A long drive snaked up a rise past ornamental saplings that

stood on quarter-acre lots. The yards hadn't been seeded yet and were bare except for some early weeds making a grab for dominance. He was suddenly terribly thirsty and wondered if the plumbing was connected in any of the models. He walked up the hill in slow strides, pacing himself against a startling fatigue that weighed him down.

The houses, each a blended design of colonial meets farmhouse meets raised ranch, looked as if they'd been built from kits and dropped from the sky. None of the houses seemed to be occupied. Richard climbed onto the porch of one and peered through the living room window.

The room was bare, except for a few dust balls and some snack food wrappers in one corner. Richard looked over his shoulder, once more checking for signs of life in the development and then turned the doorknob and stepped inside. "Hello? Anyone here?" His voice echoed against the bare walls. In the kitchen, doorless cabinets hung on a wall, and an empty recess waited for its refrigerator.

As he roamed through the rooms, delighting in the unfinished state of the house, Richard felt younger, a boy exploring abandoned structures. Upstairs, he caught sight of himself in the bathroom mirror. There was a heavy scrub of whiskers on his face and dark circles under his eyes. His hair seemed much thinner and his jawline more pronounced. He hardly recognized himself.

He strolled into an empty bedroom and looked through a dormered window at the rest of the development. Wouldn't this make the perfect place for Brady and his family? In his imagination, Richard was sure that Brady's current digs were probably quite modest, maybe a mobile home. What Brady needed was a bit of luck: a win in the lottery or an inheritance from a distant relative.

And there it was: the question of legacy. To whom would Anna and he leave their assets? The thought wearied him. He had shed all allegiances to the future, except to whatever future he and Anna could manage to carve out for themselves.

As he left the house and walked down the drive to the roadside, he wondered what a different kind of life would look like, away from the city and its pressures and demands. What if they moved out here full-time? They'd have to make an income. Anna could probably find a job in the local school district, and he could do some consulting. If they sold the co-op, they would cover their debts and make a life for themselves. With this plan brewing in his head, he nodded at an approaching car and stuck out his thumb.

17

The emptiness of the house surrounded her. Small sounds, the creak of the timbers or the rustle of bats nestled in the eaves, echoed and faded as if carried off to a more vital place. The boy was gone and along with him, a sense of fullness.

Just before dawn, she'd awakened to the sound of him padding barefoot to the bathroom. When he returned, dressed in his own clothes, he placed the neatly folded jeans and Green Day t-shirt on the seat of an armchair.

"No. That's not right." Her voice, still hoarse from sleep, startled him.

"I couldn't wash them."

"No, it's not that." Anna sat up on the sofa and lit a candle on an end table. The light cast wavering shadows as she reached for the clothes. She held them on her lap, smoothing them with her hands. "I want you to have these."

"Don't you want them?"

Anna ran her hand across the soft, worn t-shirt. "I can't tell you how many times I think I see him out of the corner of my eye. Or hear his voice in another room. I couldn't shake him if I wanted to. He's everywhere." She held the clothes out to the boy. "I think he'd like you to have these."

The boy released a deep breath. "I get it." He laid them on top of the tackle box.

"There's something else," Anna said.

"What's that?"

"This house."

"I don't want it."

"You might one day."

"I'm not staying."

"I know. I'm just saying it's yours. I'll keep it safe for you. If you ever do want it."

The boy regarded her for a long moment, as if trying to measure her intentions. Then he nodded, picked up his belongings and headed for the door. Just before he opened it, he turned back to her. "What's your name, anyway?"

"Anna. Yours?"

The boy released a hint of a smile but shook his head and said nothing as he slipped out the door.

The storm had passed; a few stars held as the night sky lightened toward dawn. Anna watched the boy—just a shadow now—walk down the long driveway and disappear around the bend. Rainwater dropped from the evergreens in an uneven staccato. The world seemed to be filled with moisture.

There were still a few live embers in the fireplace when she went back inside. Anna stirred them with the poker, placed some kindling on top of the hot spots, and blew on the embers until they flickered and caught the twigs. Just as the boy had taught her, she built a fire and leaned into its warmth as she watched the flames climb through the stories. Finally, she stood and fetched Ben's ashes from her bedroom closet.

The weight of the box always surprised her. Always so much more heft than she expected. As she knelt near the hearth and stirred the gravelly mix with her fingers, she thought of Ben's soft baby skin, the feel of his hand in hers, small and warm as they strolled through Central Park. She rolled the minute grains of crushed bones between her thumb and forefinger and thought of the weight of his infant body against her chest as she sang him to sleep. So much for his years. So much for his young muscles, for the first bristles that suggested a beard. So much for all of him, now diminished and unrecognizable in this granular reduction of a life to its elemental self: calcium, phosphate, sulfate. She placed her hand over the ashes, then picked up the pad and paper and wrote:

Somehow, Ben, I have to make my way back to the living.

She offered the note to the fire and let a lick of flame crawl up its edges and burn until she dropped it on top of Ben's ashes and watched it turn black, the paper curling and the flame dying in a wisp of smoke. As always, she stirred the paper ashes in with Ben's and returned the lid to the box.

By the time Anna went out to the garden, the sun had climbed above the tops of the pines. Bird calls charged the air as robins hunted for worms in the wet, upturned soil. As she circled the plot, she took small handfuls of ashes from the box and let a breeze carry the lightest of them away in a cloud of dust. The gravelly remains, she let drop. His atoms. They would rest and feed whatever needed feeding. This was immortality. How could the world not be haunted? It must be getting so crowded in the land of the dead. Within herself, Anna carried a little graveyard, marked with small, gray tombstones: her father, her mother, Toby, Ben, all those unknown ancestors, their headstones weathered and unreadable.

A liquid trill caught her ear, and she spotted a bird perched on a tree branch. A bright splash of red marked its shoulders as it spread its black wings and fanned its tail-feathers. A sudden spasm of joy seized her, and this joy hitched itself to a vision of the garden. Once the weather warmed, she would plant beans, carrots, tomatoes, lettuce, nasturtiums and marigolds. Crops would rise and thrive. They would be harvested until they were spent. They would shrivel and dry in late autumn's chill. They would be hoed under and disappear, joining Ben's ashes. And someday, not that far away, there would be Richard's ashes and her own, and all else that followed until all that remained was time. And once humans extinguished themselves, as Anna was sure they would, just as her own bloodline would end—a personal extinction—there would be no one left to remember anyone.

Suddenly, out of the corner of her eye, a figure moved. Someone was trudging up the driveway. A man. Older. Slower.

Richard.

The last few miles were the hardest. Richard was sweating and breathless. An ache between his shoulder blades that he'd noticed about an hour ago persisted, and his knees weren't used to this kind of exertion. His last ride had dropped him off at the village center, where everything was still closed. From there it was a steady climb up a long country road that leveled out just as it met the mouth of the driveway to the house. Then another quarter mile to get to the front door.

At first, he didn't see her. He was so tired and the ground so uneven that he kept his eyes fixed on the dirt road to keep from tripping. But after he rounded the bend, the expanse of the fields and the orchard and the open sky lifted his attention. There she was, standing by a large patch of upturned sod. She could have been a statue; she was so still, like a deer at the tree line. She was looking at him. There was something in her hands.

Just beyond Richard stood a maple tree with black leaves that gossiped with one another. Suddenly, they took to the air, and Anna saw starlings, hundreds of them. The murmuration wheeled and swooped through the air as if driven by a single, dazzling thought: *we are here.*

Anna wiped her eyes dry and looked at Richard. She took a

step toward him, then stopped. Something was wrong. He waved, then staggered a little, like a toddler. In a couple more steps his legs gave out, and he crumpled to the ground. When she realized what was happening, she dropped the box and ran.

The dew on the grass felt unbelievably comforting on his cheek. Soft and wet. Sweet-smelling, like freshly cut flowers. The pain between his shoulder blades bloomed and reached around to grip his chest. *This will pass,* he thought. *I'll just lie here for a moment.* But the moment extended and swelled until its weight pinned him to the earth, and he wondered if he would ever get up.

Soon, Anna would reach him. She would stroke his head and help him to his feet. Together, they would walk to the house. They would share coffee on the porch and watch the day brighten. Later they would stroll around the garden plot holding hands, and he would tell her everything.

Epilogue

Black pines line the road, guarding the solitude of this quiet hour. The tackle box and clothes tucked under your arm give you a sense of completion. It is peaceful along the road, and you are struck by the simplicity of life: breathe in, breathe out.

When you get to the service station, you are careful to raise the garage door quietly, slip the key from the hook, and start up the truck. Oh, how she rumbles deep in the chest, nice and steady. Even though you told your father she couldn't run, of course she could. It was a slippery little lie, and Hank swallowed it like a pelican gulps a fish.

Enough. Let him stew in your lie, along with the booze that he ran through himself over the last twenty-four hours. In the days to come, Hank will run the drink through his body until it breaks him. So, let him sleep. Let him snore the hours away until finally he wakes, bleary-eyed and dry-mouthed and finds you gone for good.

The diner in the port town was busy with the sounds of morning hunger: the clatter of plates and silverware, the trickle of coffee into cups. A bell rang twice, and the cook scolded a waitress while scrambled eggs turned to rubber under the heat lamps.

From her stool at the counter, Gina had a view of the entire dining area. There were families out for Saturday morning breakfast before ballet or hockey or just for the hell of it. At one table, a couple chatted and laughed with their kids over waffles and bacon. At another, the children ate with their eyes down while their parents looked out the window without speaking.

Gina reached into her pocket and pulled out a slip of paper: *I've gone to find the center of my universe. I hope you find yours. -R.*

That was it; nothing more. It was enough.

She carefully folded the note and tucked it into her pocket. Across the room, an elderly woman pulled a dripping tea bag out of her cup and dropped it into her husband's cup while he nodded off.

Stories. A room full of stories.

I found it, Richard. It's right here.

A bell over the entrance chimed and a man about her age walked in alone. He was tall and lanky, and he stooped as if he hoped no one would notice him. His dark hair spilled over his face, and he carried something under one arm, a green, metal box. He slid onto a stool at the opposite end of the counter and reached for the menu.

Gina studied him long enough to draw his attention and offered him a small smile. He hesitated, then smiled back. She returned her gaze to the hubbub of the diner and the richness of ordinary people living ordinary lives woven with secret dramas. The beauty of it all was almost more than she could bear.

Acknowledgments

While writing is a solitary endeavor, no one really does it by herself. I owe many thanks to many people. The members of our writers' group gave me a bounty of support, feedback, and patience. We call ourselves 'The No-Namers', but here these gifted writers shall be named: Afaa Michael Weaver, Alice Schuette, Amanda McGrew, Cherra Wyllie, Dimitri Rimsky, Emelie Burl, Fiona Demerell, Ira Morrison, Joe Connolly, Joe Matteo, Kristen Skedgell, Karen LaFleur, Merima Tranko, and Tom Lagasse. Thanks also to Fran Keilty who owns the Hickory Stick Bookshop, a gem in the crown of our little town. She gave our group a home for years. Last but far from least, a huge thank-you to Davyne Verstandig, who loves writers and does everything in her power to support them.

Once I had a decent draft, I sent it to a group of readers made up of family and friends: Davyne Verstandig, Martha Rosenthal, Bill Ratner, Andy Christie, Gerri Van Doren, and Rachelle Curry. Thank you all for your willingness to take the time to read the piece and offer helpful feedback.

I also want to thank the fine folks at Apprentice House Press, the nation's only campus-based independent publisher. As *All That Remains* is my debut novel, the process of book publication presented a steep learning curve for me. It was comforting to work with tomorrow's leaders in publication and learn along with them. I always felt that the book was in good hands.

Finally, there is David, my mate and best friend, always supportive and challenging in the best ways.

About the Author

Jane Darby's short stories, essays, and articles have appeared in *Lynx Eye, Washington Square Review, Storyglossia, Feminine Collective, New York Runner Magazine*, and *This One Has No Name*. Recently she worked as a creative consultant and researcher for the documentary film, *The Art of Eating: The Life of M.F.K. Fisher. All That Remains* is her first novel(la). She lives in rural Connecticut.

Apprentice House is the country's only campus-based, student-staffed book publishing company. Directed by professors and industry professionals, it is a nonprofit activity of the Communication Department at Loyola University Maryland.

Using state-of-the-art technology and an experiential learning model of education, Apprentice House publishes books in untraditional ways. This dual responsibility as publishers and educators creates an unprecedented collaborative environment among faculty and students, while teaching tomorrow's editors, designers, and marketers.

Eclectic and provocative, Apprentice House titles intend to entertain as well as spark dialogue on a variety of topics. Financial contributions to sustain the press's work are welcomed. Contributions are tax deductible to the fullest extent allowed by the IRS.

To learn more about Apprentice House books or to obtain submission guidelines, please visit www.apprenticehouse.com.

Apprentice House Press
Communication Department
Loyola University Maryland
4501 N. Charles Street
Baltimore, MD 21210
Ph: 410-617-5265
info@apprenticehouse.com • www.apprenticehouse.com